THE *Audacious* MISS ELIZA

THE *Audacious* MISS ELIZA

❧ DAUGHTERS OF COURAGE ❧

a regency romance by
LAURA ROLLINS

For Rob and Juli,
For the courage to put humanity on mars, and the audacity to face down cancer.

PROLOGUE

H is horse was tense, and it set Mr. Seth Mulgrave's teeth on edge. He couldn't smell anything to cause alarm—there was no smoke in the air. Still, he slowed his horse and leaned forward in the saddle slightly.

"Rachel, of course, insists the curtains are fine," Eliza said, riding beside him.

Seth reached his hand out, signaling to his daughter of three and twenty to slow as well.

Eliza pulled her horse closer to his. "Is all well?" she whispered.

Seth shook his head. "I'm not sure. Brushfire is tense."

"Starfire is at ease."

Yes, but Starfire wasn't as perceptive as her sire. Brushfire had age on his side. He may not be the fastest stallion in their stables anymore, but he knew these forested roads as well as Seth and had the experience to know when something was not right.

Like it most assuredly was now. "Stay close and be ready," he said. There was no one about besides the two of them, and there hadn't been since they'd left the small Black Hog Inn that morning.

Eliza nodded her understanding. Though her horse wasn't experienced enough to sense what Brushfire had, Eliza had accompanied him on his travels to the shops in Town often enough that she surely understood he meant to stay vigilant and be ready to bolt if necessary.

Trees lined either side of the empty dirt road, hiding what may or may not be lurking around each bend. He urged Brushfire forward once more, Eliza following a little behind.

A sound, a voice.

Seth brought Brushfire to a halt. He glanced back at Eliza. She appeared to be listening closely as well. Heaven help him, he wasn't about to allow anything to happen to his daughter. His gaze dropped to the rifle he had tethered along the packs Brushfire carried.

The voice echoed from around the next bend, finally clear enough for Seth to understand the words. "Out! Now!" The tone was clearly unrefined.

Eliza turned pale. "Highwaymen."

Seth nodded once. He gathered the reins in his hands; if they turned around now, before they were seen, they could be back to the Black Hog in a few hours. He was not about to put Eliza in harm's way.

"They're holding someone up," Eliza whispered.

She was right. The men were still shouting orders to someone—and he didn't believe they were simply ordering each other about.

"Dismount and get into the trees," he said.

Eliza quickly obeyed, and once they both had feet on the ground, they led the horses between trees and brush until they were out of sight of the main road. Seth pulled his rifle out and checked that it was loaded.

"Keep low and out of sight," he said, turning back toward the road.

"Let me come with you. I can be another set of eyes."

The devil he was going to let his daughter walk into harm's way. "Nonse—"

"I know," Eliza stopped him with a hand on his arm. The new

gloves he'd bought her as a gift from Town were a sharp contrast to the worn work jacket he wore. "That would be nonsense." She gave his arm a squeeze. "Be careful."

He leaned down, placing a quick kiss on the top of her head, and then left. Eliza was a smart, capable young woman. No doubt, if she and the horses were found, she could mount quickly and ride hard. Still, his stomach was tight at the thought of leaving her. If he found the highwaymen holding up a gluttonous popinjay, he had half a mind to leave the man be and return to Eliza. Particularly if the highwaymen had horses; most often, that meant they would take money but no lives.

After all, nothing superseded a man's responsibility to his daughters.

Seth cut through the forest as silently as he could, angling toward the shouting he'd heard moments before. As he neared, the voices grew louder.

"Open it," a man yelled. It was the same voice he and Eliza had first heard.

"If I refuse?"

That was a completely different voice—one of a refined lady. An angry, *indignant*, refined lady. Seth's steps slowed momentarily. Not a popinjay, then.

Seth slipped up behind an exceptionally wide tree and peered out onto the road. An enormous carriage with an elaborate crest emblazoned on the side rested in the center. A man who was most likely the driver knelt beside the horses, hands behind his head. There was another man—a footman perhaps?—kneeling in the same position next to him. The woman stood in a brilliant blue dress with hands on hips. Even Seth could tell her attire had not come cheaply, and he knew next to nothing about wealthy women's clothing.

A man with a hat pulled low and a cloth tied about his face and covering his mouth sauntered toward the woman. "Open the trunk, lady, or I'll *shoot* the key out of your reticule."

She gave an incensed harrumph, but at least had the smarts to start opening the reticule hanging from her wrists. Seth glanced about; two men stood in easy viewing. The one speaking to the woman, and another holding the two men at gun point. Seth lowered himself to the ground and peered beneath the carriage. The sight of a third pair of boots told him there was another high-wayman standing guard along the far side of the carriage.

Three pairs of boots total—but no horses. Seth's hand tightened on his rifle. Men who didn't have horses didn't have the means to get away easily and so often killed their victims. Devil take it all. This woman was about to lose far more than the contents of the trunk she was in the process of opening.

"They're gifts for my new grandson," she said, stepping back and letting the man paw through the contents.

"Fine gifts for a little brat. They'll garner me a pretty bit of blunt, too, when I sell 'em."

"I worked hard making those," the woman said with an obvious enough scowl, Seth could see it from where he hid.

There were no other trunks unopened near or on the carriage. It appeared the highwaymen had found everything worth taking. The three victims only had moments left. Seth lifted his gun and aimed at the man nearest the driver and footman. He already had his gun out and so would prove the most dangerous. Seth would have to take him out first. Next, he'd take out the man closest to the woman before he could harm her. The real problem would be the third man.

Seth lowered his gun slightly. He wouldn't have time to reload before he came around, and his third target no doubt had a gun out and loaded as well. His best chance would be to take the two men out and get up to the carriage before the third could come around to see what had happened. But to do that, he'd have to shoot while running.

He'd always been a bit of a bull's eye shot. Lifting his rifle back into position, he took aim once more. He could only pray today proved that yet again.

Seth let a shot ring out then darted from his covered position. Even while running, Seth swung his rifle around and sent a second bullet toward the man near the trunk. Two men down.

The horses reared and cried out but blessedly didn't bolt. The heavy sound of boots came from the other side of the carriage. The third man was heading around the back, toward Seth, the trunk, and the woman of high birth.

The woman swung toward Seth, eyes wide with shock and confusion.

"Down!" Seth yelled.

She dropped to her knees. He swung the butt of his rifle directly over her, where her head had been moments ago, just as the third man rounded the corner. The rifle butt collided with the man's temple. His head snapped back, and he dropped without a word.

Seth did a quick spin, taking in all that was around him.

The first highwayman he'd shot was now pinned down by the driver. The second was currently being tied up by the footman. The third was clearly unconscious and wouldn't be giving them any problems.

Breathing out loudly, Seth rested a hand against the carriage wheel and leaned against it. Three men down. They were all safe. Drawing in another deep breath, he found the woman staring at him.

"Pardon the interruption, my lady," he said, inclining his head. Gads, but his heart was still pumping furiously.

"Pardon you?" she said. "I think I should rather be thanking you."

He looked at her, truly looked at her, for the first time. There was a bit of gray in her hair and a few wrinkles around her eyes. But she was by no means old. More still, she appeared in no danger of fainting.

"Then perhaps your gratitude will extend far enough to excuse my bluntness. It is unwise for so fine a carriage to traverse these roads with only two men to protect it."

Seth turned, looking over his shoulder. All three men were tied up now. At least the driver and footman were competent, if not quite enough to stave off highwaymen completely.

"I do usually wait for my son before traveling," she said, her voice slowly losing the temerity of before. "Only, he has a new baby and his wife has been doing poorly since the birth." Her voice broke. "I am on my way to visit them to help, if I can." She lifted a hand to tuck back a bit of hair that had broken free from beneath her bonnet. Her hand was trembling. No doubt an effect of realizing how close she'd come to losing her life.

Seth reached a hand out. "Come; you ought to sit."

Just like that, the fire in her eyes was back, as was the indignation in her tone. "I am the Dowager Marchioness of Blackmore, and I do not cower before highwaymen or anyone."

A marchioness? Lud, he'd been certain she was of the peerage, but he hadn't realized she was *haut ton*. "Very well, my lady," he said with a low bow. "May I be of any further assistance?"

She softened, but only slightly. "I believe my men have it under control now. Many thanks to you."

"Think nothing of it."

She was a peculiar woman, one part fervor and one part heart, if he had to guess. Then again, what did a man of trade such as himself know of titled women? "If you will excuse me, my daughter is waiting for me." He pointed back toward the trees where Eliza hid. "No doubt she is worried for my safety."

"Your daughter is with you? Bring her here. I'd dearly like to meet her."

He'd much rather she not.

"I think it's best we simply be on our way," he said. It wasn't often a man from the working class gainsaid a marchioness, but after his harrowing experience, he was all the more eager to be home.

Her hands returned to her hips. "You think I'm foolish."

"No, my lady. I understand wishing to be with your family during their time of need. It is for that same reason I wish to be leaving. You see, I have two other daughters at home."

Once more, she was calm. "You wish to ascertain for yourself that they are safe."

"It is as you say, my lady." The speed at which this woman jumped from one emotion to another was enough to make any man's head spin.

"Very well," she said, drawing herself up and appearing every inch a marchioness. "I will have John see you are paid for your services, and I will bid you a good day."

"No." Seth put up his hand. "I don't accept charity." He hadn't ever. Not once in his life. He wasn't about to start now.

"This isn't charity," Lady Blackmore said. "You rendered a service. I am paying you for it."

Seth shook his head again. On this point, he was adamant.

Lady Blackmore pursed her lips. "You must allow me to show my gratitude in some manner."

"It is clear you care for your family," Seth said. "Same as I care for mine. If you will only allow me to leave to do so, I will consider that payment enough."

Lady Blackmore speared him with a look—one he was ill-equipped to understand. "I'm not comfortable with that at all. You cannot exhibit such bravery and then expect me to send you on your way." She seemed to think for a moment. "Your greatest wish is for your daughters' happiness and well-being, correct? To see them situated and safely cared for?"

What was she driving at? Any respectable father wished for nothing so much as he wished to see his daughters happy and safe. All Seth could do was nod.

Lady Blackmore smiled as if she were exceptionally pleased with herself. "Then allow me to help with *that*."

CHAPTER ONE

It had been nine months since Father had stopped the highwaymen who undoubtedly would have killed Lady Blackmore had he not.

Eliza's world had not stopped spinning since.

First, Lady Blackmore had visited; she'd insisted on meeting Mr. Seth Mulgrave's three daughters, Eliza, Rachel, and Dinah. Their neighbors hadn't stopped talking about the visit for weeks. Then, Lady Blackmore's son, the current Marquess of Blackmore, had come to visit and shake the hand of the man who'd saved his mother, grandmother to his firstborn and heir to the title. By that point, the entire town was abuzz with talk of the Mulgrave family.

Lastly, a missive came in the hands of a man who never left his name but triggered the greatest upheaval of all. The largest change in her life Eliza would, no doubt, ever experience.

Lady Blackmore had petitioned the crown, successfully, to have Father knighted.

No longer the daughter of Mr. Mulgrave who worked long hours to provide for his family, Eliza was now the daughter of Sir

Mulgrave, who was expected to remove himself from trade and set up his family with a life of comfort.

Having Lady Blackmore over yet again shouldn't have even rattled Eliza. By now, surely she should be used to such disruptions.

She wasn't.

Eliza smoothed her dress, willing her stomach to ease. Lady Blackmore's letter had said she'd be arriving sometime today, but it had given no indication of the hour. Either way, Eliza had donned her best dress. Last time Lady Blackmore had come visiting, she'd caught them all unawares. Eliza was determined to present herself better this time.

"Do you suppose she's set her cap at Father?" Dinah asked, chin pressed against an upturned fist to the point her cheek pooched out. Her blonde curls fell down across her face.

"Don't be ridiculous," Eliza muttered. A dowager marchioness interested in a man of trade? Heavens, no.

Instead of sitting up properly, or at the very least tucking her curl back where it belonged, Dinah chose to blow at the curl instead. "He is a knight now," Dinah said, pouting, likely offended her idea had been so quickly dismissed. She blew at the curl once more, but it still refused to be anywhere but directly across her face.

"A knight is hardly equal to a marchioness," Rachel added from across the room, her head still bent over her needlepoint.

She always hunched over her work when she was upset. Was it Lady Blackmore's visit she was worried about? She'd been on edge for months now, ever since the knighting ceremony. Rachel hadn't wanted to talk about it before, but perhaps Eliza should ask again. She couldn't help her sister if she didn't know what about the change in their lives was bothering Rachel.

Eliza glanced out the window; she'd chosen her seat expressly for the view it afforded her of their drive. However, since there still was no carriage, she stood and walked over to Rachel, taking the small chair beside her.

"Are you well?" she asked.

"I have no fever or cough," Rachel said, not looking up.

"That's not what I meant."

"I don't care to discuss it, then."

At least she admitted she hadn't been herself lately. "If you would only let me help you, though. Speaking of your distress may prove all you need to feel better."

Rachel shot her a quick glance before returning to her needlepoint.

Eliza sighed, looking over at Dinah.

Dinah only shrugged, the curl finally back where it belonged, and then motioned for her to press on.

"Come now," Eliza tried again. "You haven't been yourself, and I want to know why."

Rachel's needle slowed, then stopped. "You'll think me a ninny."

"No," Eliza said, placing a hand on her arm. "Of course I won't."

Rachel glanced up at Dinah.

"She won't either; will you, Dinah?" Eliza gave her sister a look which clearly let her know this was no time for teasing.

"Well . . ." Dinah drew out the word then quickly smiled. "I am only in jest. You may be many things, Rachel, but a ninny is not one of them."

Slowly, Rachel lowered her work into her lap. "Do you suppose, that is, now that Seth is a knight and on friendly terms with a marquess, that your lives will unavoidably be different . . .?"

Eliza watched Rachel closely, trying to figure out what she was saying.

"*Our* lives? There is no *us* and *you*," Dinah said. "We are family."

Rachel shook her head. "Seth is your father. Not mine."

Why would that bother Rachel now? It never had before. "His becoming a knight does not change how dear you are to us all," Eliza said. Rachel's mother, Grace Chant, was Father's younger sister. As such, when Aunt Grace's husband had been sent to Marshalsea and later died there, Rachel had come to live with them. She was more sister than cousin now. Neighbors called them "sisters" all the time, and Eliza had heard Father call her "daughter" often.

"Eliza is right," Dinah said, moving up closer to them. She knelt on the floor at Rachel's feet.

Rachel shook her head, but there were still tears lining the bottom of her lashes. "I just don't like change," she whispered. "I don't know what I'd do if I lost you two."

"Nothing will tear us apart," Eliza said, looping her arm behind Rachel's shoulders.

"We are family," Dinah said again.

Just then, the door flew open. "Never bother," came a commanding woman's voice. "I'll announce myself."

Eliza turned to see Lady Blackmore smiling as she directed several other ladies into the room behind her. "You may use that table over there," she said to one. "Only carry it a bit closer to the window first so we might see your fabric samples better."

Eliza stood, as did Rachel and Dinah. "Lady Blackmore," Eliza said with a deep curtsy.

"Oh, never mind that," Lady Blackmore said with a wave of her hand. "My daughter-in-law has that title now. I told you to call me Charlotte."

Eliza couldn't imagine calling someone as regal as Lady Blackmore by her Christian name. Never mind she was now the daughter of a knight, Lady Blackmore was still well above Eliza's station.

"Now," Lady Blackmore said, clasping her hands together and addressing the room. "Girls, this is Madame Gibbs, the finest modiste in all of England. She is here to measure you."

Dinah and Rachel stared at the small army of seamstresses before them. Eliza hated to be the one to ask the question they were all thinking, but, as oldest, it often fell to her to see things were done right. It was as Father always said: one's duty to one's family was greater than anything else.

Eliza stepped forward. "Measure us for what?"

Lady Blackmore's smile only grew. "What do you think? I have spoken with Sir Mulgrave, and I have persuaded him to bring you all to London this year for the Season." She clapped her hands at her own merriment. "You are all three to make your bows before Her Majesty and be properly introduced into society."

Eliza's jaw dropped so forcibly, it caused her cheeks to hurt.

"You cannot be serious," Dinah said.

"Can I not be?" Lady Blackmore said. "Come and look at these silks, and I'll show you how serious I am."

Tentatively, Dinah moved forward. One of the seamstresses met her in the middle of the room, several fabric swatches in her hand. "You would look fetching in the rose, miss," she said.

Eliza could not make heads nor tails of this. While Dinah eagerly looked over the fabrics and Rachel stood along the wall muttering, "I cannot like this," to herself, Eliza slipped from the room. Ever since her mother had passed due to illness when Eliza was only ten, it had been up to her to see both Rachel and Dinah well-looked after. Though Father was affluent, he worked hard to be so and was frequently gone from morning until sunset. Though they'd been able to employ a governess, Eliza had still often taken on the role of primary maternal influence. Her whole life had been about taking care of Rachel and Dinah. Only now, it suddenly felt like too much. She needed her father.

He was in his small office, sitting by the large window, likely for the light pouring into the room. Except, instead of bending low over contracts and plans, he stared out toward the front drive. If Eliza wasn't mistaken, his gaze was focused on the grand carriage parked there.

"Father?" she asked from the doorway. "Is it true?"

He rocked forward, resting his elbows atop his knees. "She told you, then?"

Eliza moved into the room. "I would much rather have heard it from you."

He ran a hand over his face. "I suppose you are right."

Eliza moved up to his desk, standing across from him. He didn't say more; he never had been one for many words. Still, couldn't he think of *something* to say at a time like this? Eliza was not as opposed to change in general, such as Rachel was, but even for her, this was growing overwhelming in the extreme.

The silence was eating at her, so Eliza finally spoke. "Are we truly going to Town for the Season?"

"Yes."

She shifted her weight. There was a chair just to her left, but she didn't feel like sitting just now; she had too many questions bottled up inside her. If only she knew how to ask them all.

"But, sir . . . why?"

When next he spoke, Father's words rushed out so fast, Eliza barely had time to make sense of them all. "To find you all husbands."

Now she did need to sit. She collapsed more than sat in the chair to her left. Her own gaze moved to the grand carriage outside. She'd had no notion that fateful morning, when she and Father had first left the Black Hog Inn, that anything would be awaiting them on the road home. She certainly hadn't thought that her entire world would pivot due to the courage of her Father that morning.

"Eliza." He said her name softly, his head finally swinging in her direction. "I need you to listen."

She nodded for him to continue.

"Nothing is more important to me than you three. Understand? Right now, I protect you. I provide for you. I keep a roof over your head and clothes on your backs." It was almost more words than he spoke on a regular day. It seemed today was full of the unexpected. "But I can't do that forever. It's time I focus on finding other men who can take on those responsibilities."

"Are you saying you're tired of dealing with three dramatic women all the time?" Eliza tried to smile, but it hurt. Moreover, it felt obviously fake.

"That's nonsense and you know it." Father stood, walked toward her, and rested back against the edge of his desk so he could face her. "I love you three too much to be so selfish as to keep you to myself any longer. Lady Blackmore has persuaded me that a London Season is the best way to see that you are all well-cared for. Permanently."

They were truly going. Somehow, she hadn't believed it until now. Still, there was part of her that seemed to fight against the idea. "Surely we cannot afford it." A London Season did not come cheap. There was a house to be rented and so many clothes to be bought. As well as the cost of moving a household, and who knew what other unexpected costs would await them once they arrived.

"Eliza," Father said, dropping to one knee, bringing himself to her eye level. "I don't want you telling this to either Dinah or Rachel." He patted her hand, pausing for a breath. "You are right. As a titled gentleman, it is expected that I stop working. It would be unseemly to continue."

Eliza knew that titled men didn't work. She secretly believed that Lady Blackmore had ascertained for herself, first, that Father had enough savings to not require he work before she'd petitioned her friends among the nobility for Father's knighthood.

"I have two options," Father said. "On the one hand, I could use what money I have saved up and buy a bit of land. I could hire others to farm it, and after five or ten years, it would be profitable enough that I would never have to work, such as befitting my new station."

That's what Eliza had been expecting they would do.

"Or," Father continued, "I could use those same funds, take us all to London, and provide my daughters the opportunity to find husbands who could provide them lives of comfort and safety."

After which he'd be left next to destitute. Eliza shook her head. "No, Father, we don't need—"

He held up a hand. "Your mother died because I could not afford to take her to Bath or bring in a better-qualified physician."

"That's not true. You did everything possible."

"Everything possible, considering our income at that time. I will not allow you three to enter in on that same road of uncertainty, not when I can prevent it."

Eliza felt her own tears start to burn against her eyes. "If we had gone to Bath or brought in a different physician, she might still have been taken from us."

"I know." He glanced away and shifted a bit. She blinked quickly; Father hated the sight of tears. "That being said, I also know there are many more gentlemen in Town who would see to it you never go hungry, who have the means to make sure you aren't cold in the winter or forced to labor all your days."

He was doing this for her—for her and Dinah and Rachel. More still, she wasn't going to change his mind. When Father decided on something, nothing swayed him. Dinah, no doubt, got her stubbornness from him. Rachel, though not his natural daughter, still managed to pick up on his natural distrust of people. If only Father was more like that now, they wouldn't be going to London.

As for Eliza, she had inherited his innate need to care for her family. Which meant, though she wasn't overly excited about this new plan, she knew she would be needed. Rachel and Dinah would struggle in London—none of them had been raised with balls and musicales in mind.

"All right," Eliza said. "Just tell me what you need from me, and I'll help in any way I can."

He gave her a rare smile. "Keep a close eye on Rachel and Dinah. They're going to need your calming influence more now than ever."

"Of course." Eliza stood, as did Father. "I best go back in there now."

She turned and made for the door, but just before walking out, she looked back over her shoulder. Father had returned to staring out the window. His life, too, had been upended ever since that morning when he'd had the courage to stop three highwaymen.

Courage.

That was another of Father's attributes. And of all the things she, Rachel, and Dinah could possibly learn from him, right now, the single virtue they needed most was courage.

CHAPTER TWO

A dam was no longer Lord Robins, as he had been growing up. As of June 28th of last year, at four in the morning—which was when his father had unexpectedly passed—he was now The Right Honorable Viscount Lambert. At least, that's what his father's solicitor had been calling him for the past eight months.

How did one reconcile with being called by a strange name? He surely ought to be used to it by now, only he wasn't. Lambert had always been his father. Adam placed his hands on either side of the small table which held his wash basin and stared at his own face reflected back at him. Was *that* Lambert? Could he possibly ever think of that man staring back at him in such a way?

Doubtful.

He pushed off the table, the wash basin rattling slightly, and stood straight. Perhaps given time.

But time was no longer on his side. Around him, where there had once been a well-covered bed, a changing room full of clothes, a hearth with a blazing fire, now instead stood folded blankets, trunks packed full, and only glowing embers. They were leaving today. He, in a dark coat, with a black band around both his sleeve and hat; his aunt, Mrs. Priscilla Bartlett, in full mourning; his cousins, Theodosia and Earnest, in subdued colors, accented with black.

A manservant walked in. "May I take the trunks out, my lord?"

Adam felt each small, imagined check on the list of things needing to happen before they left. Still, his fate could not be avoided. "Yes," he said, "let me know just as soon as the carriages are ready."

"Of course, my lord." The manservant bowed—was it just Adam, or did he bow lower now that Adam was a viscount?—and hurried to be about the work. Soon, a second and then a third manservant was also bustling about the room, picking up heavy trunks, placing Holland cloths over everything. For very nearly two decades now, this room had been his sanctuary. He could do no more than stand, dumb, watching as everything he'd ever known was covered in white.

Most likely, he would never return here; if ever he did, it would only be as a visitor. This was his aunt's home, and though he was grateful to her for raising him after his mother had passed, it was now time he stepped fully into the role that had always been meant for him. And that role could not be performed with him so far away from London.

Father had always lived in London, despite his many holdings. Now they were *Adam's* many holdings. Blast, this felt more over-whelming by the day. His solicitor, his man of business, everything was waiting for him in London.

"There you are," Aunt Priscilla said, marching quickly into the room. She forever walked and spoke vigorously, even brusquely. Growing up, Adam had always wondered if Aunt Priscilla had not been more suited to be a general than the wife of a baronet. "We are ready to depart."

"Very well," Adam said, his gaze moving over his room. It already felt foreign somehow. "The trunks are nearly all loaded on."

"Oh, never mind that," she said, moving back out of the room as quickly as she'd entered it. "They can follow behind us when they're ready. I wish to be at the inn well before nightfall. If we're going to get an early start tomorrow, we must be in bed at a timely hour tonight."

"Yes, Aunt."

She gave him a quick glance over. "Is *that* what you intend to wear today?"

Adam looked down at his tan breeches and maroon jacket. "I chose them for comfort, not for style."

"Apparently." With a shake of her head, Aunt Priscilla strode out the door.

Getting them all in the carriage and on their way was not difficult. Aunt Priscilla had spent the better part of each day these past nineteen years training Adam to be a man of consequence and decisive action. However, nothing could have prepared him for stepping into the shoes of a man he barely knew. Though he wished it otherwise, his mind would not leave his father as they rolled down the road, away from what was once his home and toward his new life. One he wasn't at all confident he was prepared for.

He'd been planning on attending London for the Season this year, even before news of his father's passing had reached him. This, the year he turned five and twenty, had always been marked as the year he would remove himself to Lambert House, the family's London townhouse, and learn directly from his father how to be a viscount.

Not that his whole life hadn't been focused on that single objective: becoming a viscount. Only, until now, his training hadn't included going to London; Father and Aunt Priscilla had been in agreement that Adam could learn more by attending University and visiting the viscount's many holdings. And it hadn't included speaking much with his father personally; they'd all believed there would be time for that.

Well, he was on his way now. But father wouldn't be waiting for him when he got there; only a stone tomb would.

The inn was nearly empty when they finally arrived. Their meal was served hot but proved to be bland. The next day's ride was much like the first. Theodosia spoke but little, Earnest and his mother filling the time with idle chatter. Adam's own gaze could hardly be pulled away from the scene outside, his mind filled with more questions than he'd had when first he'd been sent to live with his aunt after his mother passed.

But things had turned out all right then. He'd been happy living in the country, mostly. Surely, this move to London would be much the same. There would be a period of adjustment; that, he fully understood. After settling though, he'd find his bearings once more . . . wouldn't he?

Finally—or perhaps far too soon—their carriage rolled to a stop in front of Lambert House. A footman hurried forward, opening the door which Adam sat directly beside. The stucco facade of the building before them should have been familiar; after all, Adam had lived here from birth until age five. But it wasn't. He had precious few memories of his life here.

"Well," Aunt Priscilla said, "do step down and let us out."

Of course. Adam nodded and hurried down the lowered step. There was a fence about the front of the home and a railing up the stairs to the front door. A half-circle window rested above the door, with ever so many windows above that one, indicating the house boasted five stories if one included the half-basement peeking out from beneath the front step.

Aunt Priscilla pushed past him and hurried up the steps. "Where's your father's butler? He knows we're arriving today. He should have opened the door to us by now. If we walk in there and I don't find the household staff assembled to meet you, Lambert, I will advise you replace him at once."

"Yes, Aunt." She'd called him Lambert. It felt wrong to be addressed by that name. Lambert was supposed to be his father, not him.

Theodosia and Earnest walked up the stairs behind their mother while Adam continued to hang back. Just as Aunt Priscilla was lifting her hand toward the brass knocker, the door opened.

"Mrs. Bartlett," a surprisingly young man said, bowing most properly. "Please, do come in."

Was he the butler? He seemed far too young to have already risen to such a position of prestige. It was more likely he was a footman and had simply been closer to the door than the butler at the moment they arrived.

They entered the house, and, still, nothing looked familiar. Not the tiled floors nor the ornate tapestries. If Adam hadn't been entirely certain that he had lived here as a baby, he would have believed he'd never set foot inside the extravagant home.

"If you will all follow me, please." The young man bowed yet again and then turned toward the staircase which lined the wall to their right.

Adam lingered a bit, looking about him quickly. There was a library directly off to his left, and also to his left but down the corridor a bit was another room. The doors were open, and Adam strained to see what might be inside as he started up the stairs. Just before he rose too high to see anything, he caught sight of a table and chairs. The dining room, then, most likely.

As the rooms moved out of view, Adam looked up toward the space they were reaching. There was a landing, or perhaps calling it a corridor was a more accurate description. The next flight of stairs ran directly above their heads, also along the same wall. It seemed every flight of stairs in the townhouse was stacked parallel to the one below it.

As they reached the corridor, the two rooms on this floor came clearly into view. If Adam wasn't far off his mark, they were a drawing room, and just behind that a morning room.

The young man motioned with an arm toward the drawing room, allowing Aunt Priscilla, Theodosia, Earnest, and Adam to enter before him. Tall windows faced the road out front, letting in plenty of light. There, standing in a half-circle, were the staff.

Adam hazarded a glance at Aunt Priscilla; so he apparently wouldn't need to be replacing the butler after all.

The young man began introductions, but Adam lost track almost immediately. His head was swimming too much with the house and the unavoidable knowledge that this would be his new home—strange though it was—to stay focused on names. At least he was able to hold on to the name of the housekeeper, Mrs. Simmons. The young man ended by introducing himself as Mr. Reid, the butler.

If Aunt Priscilla's raised brow was any indicator, she was as surprised as Adam. He'd never known someone so young to be a butler. However, he didn't want to cause too much upheaval on his first day as master of Lambert House, so Adam didn't question the man's position.

How odd to think that now Adam had authority over Mr. Reid's position. His gaze moved across the many faces looking back at him. Over all their positions.

"Well," Aunt Priscilla said once the introductions were done. "I, for one, am quite exhausted from our travels. Mrs. Simmons, if you will show us to our rooms, I am sure we could all use a rest and some time to freshen up before dinner."

"Of course, my lady," Mrs. Simmons said with a curtsy. "Only . . . well"—her gaze jumped to Mr. Reid, to Aunt Priscilla, and finally to Adam—"we were not sure where you wanted everyone placed, my lord."

He didn't know why she was looking at him; he certainly had no idea where everyone ought to be placed. He had no notion how many bedchambers the house boasted or how comfortable they might be.

"I am sure," he said to Mrs. Simmons, "whatever you believe to be best will suit us fine for now." Hopefully, he wasn't putting his faith in the wrong person. He had no notion of the kind of staff his father had employed. Lud, but he had a lot to figure out. At least the housekeeper appeared to be the age of most women of her station.

"Yes, thank you, your lordship," Mrs. Simmons hedged. "You wouldn't mind Mrs. Bartlett taking the room opposite yours, then? The one your mother once used?"

Adam's brow dropped. Having a visitor take the mistress's room was odd indeed.

"That will be unnecessary," Aunt Priscilla said. "There are three guest chambers; one for each of us." She motioned to Adam's cousins.

Mrs. Simmons clutched her hands in front of her. "Yes, my lady, only the one furthest back is the nursery."

Aunt Priscilla waved off the dilemma. "Theodosia will not mind a few nights in a nursery once more."

Still, Mrs. Simmons did not seem satisfied. "Yes, my lady, but Miss Kitty is currently occupying the nursery."

"Who?" Aunt Priscilla asked.

"His lordship's"—she turned to Adam once more—"*your* ward."

Adam's stomach flipped. "Come again?"

"Your ward, my lord. The late Lord Lambert took her in as a baby and promised he'd look after her all her days." The housekeeper drew herself up. "She'll be your responsibility now." Mrs. Simmons's last statement was firm, brooking no disagreement.

A *ward*? When the blazes had that happened? Adam slowly turned toward his aunt. She looked as stunned as he.

"There must be some mistake," Aunt Priscilla said. "My brother-in-law has no ward."

"Begging your pardon," Mr. Reid said, stepping forward. "But he did, and now, so does his lordship." The butler looked over at Adam with the same expectant look Mrs. Simmons had given him. Whoever this Miss Kitty was, she clearly had the entire household on her side.

Everyone was staring at him. Not only his aunt and cousins, but the entire staff was watching him, waiting to see what he would do now. Adam was rather made to believe that, should he choose to throw Miss Kitty out, he'd have a coup on his hands.

"Well," Adam began, "I suppose I ought to meet Miss Kitty." Mrs. Simmons—indeed the entire staff—continued to eye him, as though assessing if they would need to oust him or not. "That is," Adam added, "if she is to be living here under my roof."

That seemed to calm the impending mob.

"Very well, my lord," Mrs. Simmons said. "I'll have her governess bring her down."

Oh, so not *all* the staff had been gathered after all. Apparently, his authority over the household was not to be assumed.

Mrs. Simmons curtsied once more and then hurried out the

door. Her footsteps sounded from the stairs. Adam glanced over at his aunt and cousins. They only continued to stare back. The silence quickly grew awkward. Of all the things he'd imagined finding upon arriving at Lambert House as its master, a ward had never been one of them.

Mrs. Simmons returned, a woman of indeterminate age following behind with a young girl holding tightly to her hand.

"My lord," Mrs. Simmons said, pointing toward the girl, "this is Miss Kitty."

She could not have been more than six, *quite* young to already have a governess instead of a nursemaid. And so petite. Her blonde hair was set in perfect curls about her face with a light blue ribbon to offset it. Her dress was clearly well made and her slippers, which peeked out from beneath her hem, were dotted with beads. Apparently, his father had spared no expense when it came to this little girl.

Adam moved over until he stood directly in front of her. She looked up at him, her eyes wide. Though, if he had to guess, there was more curiosity in her gaze than fear.

He dropped to one knee, coming to eye level with her. "Good day to you, Miss Kitty. I am Lord Lambert."

Her brow creased. "No, you're not. Lambert died."

Not overly shy then, was she?

"I'm sorry, my lord," the governess said. "I have tried to explain to her."

"Don't worry about it." He turned back to Miss Kitty. "The Lord Lambert you knew was my father. And you're right, he has passed on. Now, I carry his name."

"And you get the house," Miss Kitty said, "and all the servants . . . and me."

Apparently some of what her governess had said actually had sunk in. "That's correct."

Miss Kitty listed her head. "Will you buy me ribbons for my hair, too?"

Adam smiled. "Certainly."

He had no notion where this little girl had come from, or what she'd been to his father, or how he was going to manage this unexpected responsibility, but after only a few short sentences between them, Adam knew full well he'd be watching over the girl from now on.

CHAPTER THREE

E liza reached across the carriage bench and straightened one of
the flowers in Dinah's blonde hair.

"Thank you," Dinah said, straightening another one. "I swear I
look far more nervous than I actually am."

"That's because I did your hair, not you," Eliza said, looking
over all the flowers carefully. "And I'm as nervous as one can be." As
a little girl, she'd often dreamed of making her bows. Only, when
the moment had actually come four days prior, Eliza had found it
not at all to her liking, despite Lady Blackmore's many hours of
instruction. There had been so many people, all of them staring at
her and her family.

"You really ought not fret," Dinah said, gently pushing Eliza's
hands away. "You look as lovely as ever."

Rachel, who sat across from them and beside Father, gave Eliza
a half-smile. "You truly do look lovely." Which was exactly how
Eliza would have described Rachel, whose dark hair had been piled
high on her head and accented with dozens of pearls. Her square-
necked dress was most becoming, flattering her curves and accentu-
ating her long neck.

Eliza rested back against the squabs. She didn't feel ugly at the moment. But she was less concerned with her looks and more concerned with how many stares she'd be receiving tonight.

It was their first ball; Lady Blackmore had insisted they enter society with something of a splash, and that meant not at some simple, small dinner party. How did one even act during a ball? Though her governess had taught her how to behave at a country assembly, and Lady Blackmore had spent several mornings instructing her, Dinah, and Rachel on grace and poise, standing now among the glittering upper echelon, Eliza couldn't help but feel all her education inadequate. Did Lady Blackmore truly understand how unprepared Eliza was for a life among the *ton*?

She glanced at her three traveling companions. At least she wouldn't be facing this trial alone. She'd never been so thankful for her family in all her life.

The carriage rolled to a stop, but Father was up and had the door open before the waiting footman could approach. Father hopped down and then lowered the steps himself, turning his back toward the footman. The manservant, for his part, simply watched on, clearly unsure how to treat a superior who wouldn't let him do his job.

Lady Blackmore had helped Father find servants and staff members aplenty. In the end, Father had agreed to hire but a few hands—a butler, a groomsman, two footmen, a housekeeper, a lady's maid, and two maids-of-all-work. It felt like ever so many people just for the four of them. Still, according to Lady Blackmore, it wasn't nearly enough. The number they had employed was something of a compromise between their benefactress's wishes and Father's pride. Eliza rather guessed Father's pocketbook did have something to say about how many individuals they employed.

Though, was it more about his pocket book, or his pride? Eliza glanced at her Father as she stepped out of the carriage, the last of them to disembark. His back was ramrod straight and still turned toward the uncertain footman. Eliza took her father's hand and let him help her down.

His pride. Even more than his decidedly practical pocket book, Father tended to make decisions based on his pride.

"Have you ever seen anything so lovely?" Dinah asked.

Eliza let her gaze move up and take in the whole of the house. It was well-lit with what must have been hundreds of candles. "Where does one even find the time to trim all those wicks and then light them one by one?"

Rachel nodded. "To say nothing regarding putting them all out, packing them away in a manner to prevent them snapping, and then polishing the candlesticks later."

Dinah only pursed her lips and shook her head at them. "What a couple of gooses you are. That's what maids are for." Out of all of them, Dinah seemed to be handling this sudden upheaval in their life the best.

"I know that," Rachel said. "Only a few months ago, however, we were more suited to the *company* of all those maids."

"We were never so poor as all that," Eliza said. They hadn't titles or land to boast of, but they'd been well-off for having a father in trade. She didn't voice so much aloud though, for undoubtedly if she did, Rachel would remind her that being well-off for having a father in trade was nothing compared to the situation they now found themselves in.

"Only think," Dinah said with a bright smile, "*we* shall be dancing with the gentlemen of the *ton* tonight."

Eliza couldn't find the excitement her sister seemed to emanate. Holding tightly to one another, the three women followed Father through the doorway and into the glorious house. It was even more opulent inside. Everything had clearly been freshly polished. Floors, railings, even chairs all shone softly in the candlelight. They moved up the stairs, the sounds of a talented orchestra guiding their way.

Lady Blackmore awaited them at the top of the stairs.

"There you are," she said loudly enough to garner much attention. "I had almost given up hope of seeing you all tonight."

Eliza kept her gaze on Lady Blackmore, but she couldn't fully ignore the fact that *many* pairs of eyes were on them.

"Good evening," Father said, bowing before Lady Blackmore. She gave him a curtsy and then turned toward Eliza, Rachel, and Dinah.

"You all look lovely," she said.

Eliza had always thought of Lady Blackmore as a handsome woman. But tonight, in her dark-blue silk gown with cream-colored feathers in her hair, she was far more. She was distinguished, she was elegant. Lady Blackmore *belonged*—and Eliza felt keenly that she did not.

"Well, come along." Lady Blackmore hurried them forward.

The ballroom was no less grand or intimidating. From the chalked floors to the chiffon-draped ceiling, it was perfection. The people inside, too, were far more lovely than anything Eliza had ever before beheld. The superfine jackets, the gowns and feathers.

Eliza held more tightly to Rachel; she would not faint. She was determined not to.

The next two hours challenged her resolve. She met ever so many people—gentlemen, ladies, matrons. Her head would not stop swimming. Worse still, as the oldest, it was as though most individuals expected her to carry the majority of the conversation. Even after Lady Blackmore had made their excuses and they'd moved on to another small group of people, Eliza would feel the gazes following her.

She couldn't help but overhear their whispers, too.

"Have you heard the tale?"

"Sir Mulgrave is quite the hero."

"All three girls out at once?"

"Quiet, mousy little things, all of them."

"Still smell of the shop, if you ask me."

Eliza slowly shut her eyes and took a fortifying breath as Lady Blackmore introduced them to a Lord and Lady Honeyfield and their daughter, Lady Augusta. The daughter seemed close to Eliza's own age, with perfectly set blonde curls framing her face and light blue eyes, though there was no red in her curls as there was in Dinah's. Her smile appeared sincere. The small amount of genuine pleasure eased Eliza's tense stomach somewhat.

"Is it not the most extravagant ball you've ever seen?" she asked Eliza.

"It is," Eliza replied, feeling about as graceful as a colt among thistles.

"I do believe nearly all of London is here tonight," Lady Augusta said, her eyes wide with excitement.

The thought only made Eliza's stomach tighten once more. She wasn't ready for this. She hadn't the years of training and preparation same as all these women. Eliza didn't hear much of the conversation.

After expressing her pleasure at meeting them all, Lady Augusta moved off with her parents. With the room spinning about her, Eliza told Lady Blackmore she would like some punch and slipped off before the lady could disagree. She was typically fine when conversing with or meeting new people, particularly in small, intimate gatherings. Speaking one-on-one with nearly anyone, she could manage. But there were ever so many people here, it undid her. The punch table was only a few strides away, but when she reached it, the small drink didn't feel nearly enough. What she needed was a breath of fresh air. But the doors to the outside balcony were closed. She couldn't blame the owners; it was frightfully cold outside, after all. Still, her gaze remained on the doors. If only she could be free, if only for a moment.

Next to the doors and off to the right was a small alcove, almost completely covered by curtains. Eliza put her empty cup down and moved toward it. This corner of the ballroom was not nearly as packed with people, and those who were here focused on the dance floor and not on her.

Eliza inched her way back, back, closer and closer to the alcove. No one appeared to be watching her or looking her direction at all. With one last glance about, she hurried the last few steps and slipped in behind the curtains. Pressing her back against the cold wall, Eliza breathed deeply.

The unexpected moment of solitude was freeing.

Slowly, she sunk down until she was sitting. Heavens, but it felt good to be alone, even if she knew it could only be for a minute. Eliza tipped her head back. And to think, this was only her *first* ball.

How many more awkward, blundering moments was she to have while here in London?

⚜

Adam looked about the ballroom but barely saw it.

He had a ward.

The thought still shocked him. It still occupied nearly every second of his waking time. He'd been staying at Lambert House for nearly a week now, so he'd had much time to get to know Miss Kitty. But the knowledge that he was personally responsible for her—for her education, for her safety, for her future—still felt strange. Probably would for quite some time yet.

"I do appreciate a well-chalked floor," Aunt Priscilla said from where she stood near his elbow. They had finally decided on the best place for everyone to stay while at Lambert House. The townhouse had a total of five bedrooms; the master's bedchamber and the mistress's bedchamber were both on one floor, with three bedchambers on the floor above, one of which was the nursery. The only option they'd been able to see their way to was to give Theodosia and Earnest rooms on the top floor and have Aunt Priscilla stay in the mistress's room beside his own.

"Yes, Aunt." Perhaps if he could figure out Miss Kitty's relationship to his father, that would help.

"I still say you should have worn your dark blue jacket. It fits you much better than this one."

"If you say so." He didn't feel he could ask either the defensive Mrs. Simmons or the unexpectedly young Mr. Reid about Miss Kitty's history. How would that sound, to have the master of the house confess his own naivety regarding something so vital? Not to mention sensitive. Though there had been nothing near insubordination since his arrival, he had caught several glances and whispered conversations between servants that all hinted they didn't truly view him as their master. To ask about Miss Kitty would certainly only undermine his authority in their eyes. And he certainly couldn't ask Miss Kitty.

"Come now, you've been far too quiet all week," Aunt Priscilla said. "It's time you stopped all this woolgathering and attended to the ladies here tonight."

Adam chuckled softly—anyone would be consumed with "woolgathering" had they suddenly found themselves responsible for a little girl.

Could she possibly be his half-sister? It seemed the most likely reason his father had taken responsibility for her. Still, Adam was certain no one had ever mentioned his father remarrying. Not that that meant the late Lord Lambert couldn't have had another child. If that was the case, he best not ask Mrs. Simmons, nor Miss Notley; he had no desire to offend either woman's sensibilities.

"Oh, for heaven's sake," Aunt Priscilla said, whirling around and facing him. "I am done with your silence. I am going to take one of the seats over by Lady Honeyfield. I expect to see you dancing most sets."

"I cannot dance," Adam protested, indicating the black band about his arm. "The time of my mourning has not yet passed." Aunt Priscilla was usually such a stickler for formalities.

Instead, she only huffed. "Then I shall expect to see you *speaking* with several different young women throughout the night."

Adam glanced about the room, forcing himself to actually see it this time. "But I hardly know a lady present."

"You know enough people here to manage, I am sure." She gave him no more help than that before spinning on her heel and marching off.

Very well, it was apparently up to Adam to find an acquaintance or two who might provide introductions. Across the room, he saw someone he thought he knew, a gentleman he'd attended university with. Adam took a few steps to his left, taking his time in making his way around the room.

The thing was, if Miss Kitty was Adam's half-sister, then where was her mother? He'd known men to turn out mistresses after a time. But what man turned away his mistress, but continued to house and feed his child? It didn't make sense. Unless his father had been touched in the head.

It was immensely disconcerting to admit, albeit only to himself, that Adam hadn't know his own father well enough to know if he had been a bit mad. Imagine if he asked Mr. Reid.

Pardon me, but could you tell me if my own father was perhaps headed toward Bedlam?

The butler would either laugh in his face or decide he was a fool. Adam shook his head at his own ignorance as he paused near the punch table and picked up a drink. He'd written his father many times growing up, and his father had often written back. But he'd only come to visit Adam a couple of times. Now that he'd taken time to think it over, letters were a pitifully ineffectively way of getting to know a person. Was his father one to keep a mistress? He'd never wondered before coming to London. Aunt Priscilla had always spoken highly of his father but had rarely provided any detail. Adam had been led to believe the man had been well-respected by all.

He glanced over at his university acquaintance. The man had moved in the opposite direction, away from Adam. It was just as well; Adam wasn't much in the mood for light conversation just now anyway. Turning his back to the ballroom, he walked toward the closed balcony doors. But instead of the wintry scene outside, he saw only his wavy reflection, one that grew as he neared it. Was *that* Lord Lambert anything like his father? How would he even know? Suppose—

His foot caught on something and, wrapped up as he had been in his own thoughts, he hadn't the wherewithal to do anything more than catch himself on his hands and knees. The small cup of punch he carried clanked as it hit the floor then rolled away.

What the blazes had he tripped over? Aunt Priscilla had been on his case all day regarding how distracted he'd been, but this was ridiculous. Adam glanced over to his right. A young woman, sitting just off to his right, stared back at him.

"I am so sorry," she said quickly, pulling her feet yet further beneath her; no doubt, it was her feet he'd tripped over.

Adam hurried to stand, offering his hand out to the lady. "I'm the one who must apologize. I should have watched where I was stepping." Clearly, he'd been more lost in thought than even he had realized, to have done something so imbecilic as trip over a lady's feet.

"Oh?" She slipped her hand into his, and he helped her stand. "Is it often you must keep a look-out for the stray slipper?" She was wearing a simple ball gown, nothing nearly as ornate as he'd seen on most women in attendance. Still, the cream fabric with a blush pink organza over the top was quite becoming. It complimented her figure while drawing out the deep brown in her eyes.

Lud, he was staring. Adam laughed lightly even as he felt his face warm. "As a gentleman, I've been taught it is my duty to keep out for a stray anything." Was that what Miss Kitty had been to his father? No more than a stray girl in need of protection?

The young woman laughed, and the sound, full and genuine, brought him back to the present. "I suppose when there are ninnies like me about, one *does* have to keep an eye out."

She'd been hiding back behind the curtain; that's why he hadn't noticed her before tripping over her. Was she shy? Or simply over-whelmed?

Adam motioned toward the swirling crush. "It can be a bit much, can't it?"

Her shoulders slumped a bit. "Ever so much so."

"My cousin would agree if she were here." While Earnest had been upset at not being allowed to attend, Theodosia had only breathed a sigh of relief. "She likes to keep to herself and prefers small gatherings to large ones like this."

"I believe she and I would find much we agree upon."

Adam opened his mouth to say he, too, often found balls like this overwhelming. Before he could, the lady seemed to catch sight of someone.

"Pardon me, but it appears I have been missed." With nothing more than that, she hurried off. She did cut quite a lovely figure. All too soon, Adam lost sight of her between a group of matrons.

Strange encounter, that had been. The woman had appeared out of thin air, tripped him most unceremoniously, engaged him in a lovely chat, and, almost as quickly, vanished.

He stared after the spot where he'd last seen her. Theodosia probably would have a lot in common with the lady—whomever she was. Adam moved away from the alcove and back toward the refreshment table. He shouldn't have carried on a conversation with her, seeing as they hadn't been introduced. But he hadn't felt he could help her to her feet and simply rush off. Or perhaps he simply hadn't wanted to.

Adam shook his head. She was gone now, regardless. London was such a massive place, with so many people forever coming and going, there was a real chance he'd never see her again. He'd simply have to add her to his growing list of *Surprising Experiences Had In London*. Miss Kitty came forcibly back to mind. Right now, that list was growing longer by the day.

CHAPTER FOUR

E liza wrapped an arm through Rachel's. "Cheer up. A visit with Lady Honeyfield and her daughter won't be all that bad." After all, the sun was shining that morning, the snow had melted along the walks and roads, and though it was still February, it was a mild cold that filled the lungs with energy rather than attack them with a biting chill.

Still, Rachel shook her head, her bonnet wiggling unsteadily.

Eliza pulled her cousin to a stop, tugging on the bonnet's ribbons and then retying them more securely. "We shall have a pleasant time. I promise."

They once more began walking, Lady Blackmore and Dinah just ahead of them. But Rachel remained silent. She had a tendency to pull into herself, to remain silent and complaisant. But that didn't mean she was happy.

It was time Eliza tried a more direct approach. "I am sure your mother is fine."

Rachel's voice was barely more than a whisper. "I miss her."

"Of course you do, as I'm sure she misses you." Eliza hugged Rachel's arm closer to her. "But she wouldn't want you fretting your Season away, worried over her."

"But I don't know if she truly *does* miss me."

Oh. Eliza's steps slowed. "Of course she misses you."

Rachel's eyes were sad. "Then why doesn't she write?"

Aunt Grace hadn't written her own daughter? When Eliza hadn't received word back, she'd assumed Aunt Grace was either too busy to reply or, more likely, didn't have the coin necessary to send each of them a letter. But she'd always believed Aunt Grace had written Rachel back.

"Eliza?" Lady Blackmore called back. "Rachel?"

Eliza faced forward once more. She hadn't realized how far behind Dinah and Lady Blackmore they'd fallen. Eliza gave Rachel's arm one more squeeze and then they hurried forward.

"Now," Lady Blackmore began the moment Eliza and Rachel caught up. "Lady Honeyfield mentioned the other night that her oldest daughter won't be joining them here in London for another couple of months due to illness. However, Lady Augusta has had her coming out and has already drawn interest from several gentlemen. Some of whom *may* be in attendance today during our visit."

Eliza certainly hoped not. She never knew who she ought to be around ladies of such an elevated station. Having gentlemen present only made things all the harder. Eliza had made morning calls before, but they'd never felt as formal, as rule-bound, as they had since Father was knighted.

"Remember," Lady Blackmore continued, "it is inconsiderate to draw *too* much attention from the men when they've come to visit another woman. However, I gathered from Lady Honeyfield that the family is more concerned that their eldest make a good match this year. Lady Augusta is here more to enjoy herself. So, drawing *some* attention to yourself would not be unseemly."

Some days, it felt like Lady Blackmore's instructions never ceased. Then again, there was ever so much for them all to learn.

Dinah gave Eliza a saucy smile. "That means you might have to stay where people can actually see you."

"Oh, come now," Eliza muttered. They'd hardly stopped teasing her ever since she'd stepped away for a moment to herself during the ball last week.

Not that she'd been alone for much of the time. The gentleman she'd spoken with, after accidentally tripping him, had turned out to the best part of the evening. He, at least, had been sincere and kind. Handsome, too. Had it been terribly naughty that she'd kept an eye out for him the rest of the night? But their paths had never crossed again; pity, that. Then again, during her brief conversation with Lady Augusta, the woman had also seemed sincere and kind. Perhaps this morning's visit would show her to be so again.

"Rachel, Dinah, you two walk ahead. I want to speak with Eliza."

Botheration. Eliza didn't for a minute think Lady Blackmore wanted to speak to her to tell her all the things she'd done right since coming to London. Lady Blackmore was no dragon, but she didn't turn a blind eye either.

Dinah and Rachel did as they were told and were soon several paces ahead.

"Your sister is right, you know."

Eliza nodded.

"You seem to grow more anxious the larger the gathering."

"An astute observation." It hadn't been much of a problem for Eliza before, but now they were forever in large gatherings, and she couldn't escape the feeling she was being judged by every pair of eyes.

"Is it that you feel unequal to the company?" Lady Blackmore asked. "Or simply overwhelmed?"

"Both, I imagine."

"London can be a vast and intimidating experience."

"Especially for one who was not raised to live like this."

Lady Blackmore's boots scraped against the walk as she came to an abrupt stop and turned to face Eliza. "Do you not wish for such a life?" There was no superior huff in her tone, only an honest desire to understand.

Eliza stopped as well, taking the time to truly look at Lady Blackmore. The marchioness wore a rich purple pelisse trimmed with fur. Her hair was done up and surrounded by a dignified turban. It was by far the most elegant attire Eliza had ever seen anyone wear for a simple morning call. But a woman like Lady Blackmore never had to worry about whether or not she'd stay warm during the winter, if her clothes were wearing holes in the elbows, or if there was enough in the pantry to last through the week. It was a far gentler life than the one Eliza had always envisioned for herself.

Did Eliza want a life such as hers?

"Yes," she said. "Of course I do." But her words lacked conviction.

Lady Blackmore's smile tugged to the side. Apparently, Eliza was fooling no one. "Let me ask you this. Had you any friends growing up? People whose company you enjoyed?"

"A few, yes."

"Who?"

The rows of houses to either side of them blurred as Eliza thought back. "There was Mary; we were very good friends when I was about eight. And there were a couple of girls when I was fourteen, and we all got along quite well."

"Why did you like them?"

"They were polite, honest. They listened when I spoke, and we often agreed with one another on various topics."

"Do not forget Dinah and Rachel. I had only known the three of you five minutes before I knew full well you three are quite close."

Eliza's smile softened at the thought of her family, her gaze jumping ahead to where they walked. "Yes, I have been very blessed to have them."

"And they, to have you."

Eliza only shrugged. She did try as much as she was able to help and comfort Dinah and Rachel.

"Were there ever any young men who caught your eye?"

Eliza's cheeks warmed. "Oh, I doubt . . ."

Lady Blackmore eyed her pointedly. "Come now, a beautiful young woman like yourself?"

"Well . . ." Eliza had never spoken of this to anyone, not even Rachel or Dinah. But Lady Blackmore was easy to confide in.

"There was one gentleman." The young Mr. Collin. She hadn't pulled out his memory and turned it over in years.

"I'm not at all surprised."

"I was far too young, only barely fourteen."

"Some matches begin at that age."

"I suppose. We spoke a few times with one another is all, but I did think he rather fancied me." They were sweet memories. Their attachment had been brief and not enough to cause a broken heart when it ended.

Taking her arm, Lady Blackmore started them walking once again. "What happened?"

Eliza smiled to herself. Though she hadn't known Lady Blackmore long, they'd been in company enough ever since that fateful May day that she knew the woman quite well now. She ought to have known Lady Blackmore wouldn't have let the subject go without knowing the details.

"He joined the Navy," Eliza explained. "His ship was sent to the continent, and soon after, his family quit the neighborhood. I never heard what happened to him." That was several years ago now. What *had* happened to him? She hoped he was home, safe, and happy.

"So you are telling me," Lady Blackmore said, "that you've had many friends, and even drawn the notice of a man you would have liked to know better?"

"Yes, I suppose I am."

Lady Blackmore took Eliza's hand. "Then don't assume you can't do the same here in London."

The words were comforting, but Eliza wasn't convinced. "But back home, I was where I belonged. I was among my equals."

"First rule of London: don't listen to any of the lofty drivel or pretentious nonsense half the people here spout as truth. Your father is a knight. You are a respectable woman. You belong."

"I'm still the same woman I was before my father stopped those highwaymen."

"In essence, you have not changed, Eliza dear, but don't doubt that being who you always have been is a very good thing."

"I don't think people here in London will see it that way."

"They will. The ones who matter will, anyway. Trust me. I've seen enough of London to know. There will always be naysayers and critics. But I say, let them consume themselves with their own contempt. You remember that; just as you found individuals whose company you enjoyed in the past, you can find them here, too."

As it happened, there were no gentlemen present. Spurred on by the small bit of relief such a realization brought, Eliza determined to hold on to Lady Blackmore's words—she could find friends here, too. After all, she'd hate for someone to judge her based on how she'd grown up or what she might be wearing that day; it would certainly be wrong for her to do the same to others by assuming they wouldn't care for her or make good companions. Most of the people who sat in Lady Honeyfield's morning room certainly had grown up differently than Eliza, and most were wearing far lovelier dresses. Still, Eliza was determined to give them a chance. She would not be found guilty of assuming their differences meant they wouldn't be pleasant company.

"And how are you finding London, Miss Eliza?" Lady Augusta asked.

If ever there was a chance to take Lady Blackmore's words to heart, it was now. Eliza placed her teacup down and turned herself to face Lady Augusta a bit more, as those sitting around them carried on a different conversation.

"I find it pleasing . . ."

Lady Augusta pinned her with a look.

"And a bit overwhelming," Eliza confessed.

"Only a bit?" Lady Augusta asked, her voice dropping lower. "I have been quite beside myself. Jane, my sister, has told me all about her previous Seasons. She's had *four*. But not even her detailed accounts were enough to prepare me."

Eliza felt a bit of the tightness insider her ease. "It is all rather a bit much, isn't it?"

"I'll say." Lady Augusta picked up a small bit of honey cake. "But wasn't the ball last week elegant?"

"It was surely the most exquisite thing I've ever seen."

"Me too," Lady Augusta agreed. "I'd heard about how lovely balls often are, but the country assemblies I've been too fairly paled in comparison."

Eliza's shoulder's relaxed. Apparently, she hadn't been the only one surprised at the splendor that night. Lady Blackmore was right; Eliza wasn't so out of her sphere as she'd originally assumed.

"After all your sister has told you," Eliza said, "what events are you most looking forward to?"

Lady Augusta took a bite and chewed for a minute. "A ride through Hyde Park has always struck my fancy. Though it's not mother's idea of an enjoyable time, so I may have to wait for a gentleman to ask me."

"Why not go on your own?"

Lady Augusta's eyes grew wide. "Oh, I don't know if I dare."

"I don't mean *alone*." Even Eliza knew better than that. "Of course you'd take a manservant with you. Only, it might not happen if you don't make it."

"I suppose one can't always rely on a gentleman being on hand to do one's bidding." Lady Augusta giggled.

"Augusta," Lady Honeyfield called.

Both she and Eliza looked up. Lady Honeyfield didn't look too pleased at hearing her daughter laugh so loudly.

"Lady Blackmore and I would care for a short turn through the gardens," she said, shooting Eliza a disapproving look. Apparently, it was her fault Lady Augusta had made a sound far too loud to be ladylike. "It hasn't been this warm in months, and we'd hate to waste it."

Lady Augusta readily agreed and then turned toward Eliza, either inclined to ignore her mother's disapproval or oblivious to it. "Does that sound pleasant to you?"

Eliza hadn't meant to be a poor influence on her new friend. She would have to try harder to not be so again in the future. As for an outing, nothing sounded better. After being so often stuck indoors, she was ready for hours and hours outside. However, as she caught a glance at Dinah, her agreement died on her lips.

Though Dinah's eyes were cast down, she did not look at ease with the idea of taking a stroll. Which was odd, for Dinah liked being outside nearly as much as Eliza.

Rachel caught her eye and silently mouthed, "New boots."

They were all wearing new boots—it was part of the ever-growing pile of clothes and items Lady Blackmore insisted they have for their Season. Eliza's feet were fine, but suppose Dinah's had not been as accurately measured? New boots could be quite uncomfortable the first several times one wore them. They had already walked quite far today.

Eliza turned back to Lady Augusta. "If it's all the same to you, I thought I might sit for a bit. Perhaps enjoy the view from your windows."

"Are you certain?"

Eliza hesitated. She would miss not being outside. She longed for some more time in the sun, and who knew when it would be bright outside once more?

A quick glance at her sister settled the matter though. "Yes, quite certain. Dinah and I shall be quite happy in here for the time being."

Dinah's look of relief was immediate.

"Very well. If you are certain," Lady Augusta said, standing.

Eliza moved over to sit beside Dinah as the ladies filed out of the room with promises to return in only a few minutes.

Once the door closed behind them, Dinah took Eliza's hand. "Thank you. I couldn't stand to do any more walking at this point, not while knowing we'll have to walk home."

"Are they pinching that badly?"

"I'm afraid so. I shall give them another chance after today, but if they don't loosen up, I shall have to replace them."

The boots had been quite expensive. Eliza hated the thought of Father paying for yet another set. Though it was Lady Blackmore's taste they relied on, it was, nonetheless, Father who was paying for it all. Though his savings had been sizable for a man of his station, such a sum was small compared to what most *haut ton* families spent in a single Season. "Perhaps if we trade?"

"Excuse me?"

"Mine aren't pinching at all, and our feet are very nearly the same size."

Dinah rocked back. "Are you making fun of my big feet again?"

"No, believe me. I am in earnest. If yours are too small for you, it only makes sense I should wear them."

"Because *you* don't have such big feet. Is that what you mean?" Though Dinah argued, she was already removing the offensive footwear. Eliza hurried to take her boots off as well.

With a sigh, Dinah tugged the second off and wiggled her toes. "Do you think anyone will notice we've switched?"

"Probably not." Eliza held one of her boots out to her sister.

Dinah took the boot with a giggle. "We should make it a game. Every time we go somewhere, part way through, we'll switch something. Bonnet, reticule, shawl, something. Then, we'll wait to see if anyone notices."

It did sound like fun. "I'm only worried what we would say if someone did catch us."

Dinah pulled on one of Eliza's boots. "We could play it one of two ways. We could either laugh it off and call it a silly game between sisters, or we could act innocent and pretend we haven't any idea what they're talking about."

That sounded like it would only draw more attention and cause ever so much confusion. "I like the first idea better."

"I was worried you'd say that. I prefer the second." Dinah sat back, stuck her feet out, and rested her heels against the floor where she might see her new boots. "I may change my mind after walking home, but for now, these are fitting far better."

Eliza pulled on Dinah's boots. They *were* snug. Though Eliza never said as much—Dinah laughed about it, but she was sensitive about her feet—Eliza's feet were smaller than her sister's. Not by much. Still, if these boots were snug on Eliza, they certainly must have been biting on Dinah.

"Are you sure you will be all right with those?" Dinah asked.

"Yes, I will be fine."

Dinah pressed her lips into a tight line. "Now, don't go saying how those boots provide more than enough room for your feet—you'll only make me feel like a giant, monstrous goose with the largest feet ever seen."

"Very well. They are a bit tight," Eliza confessed.

However, instead of looking pleased, Dinah only rested back more fully and shook her head. "Eliza, you are in for a life of sorrow, I fear."

Eliza shifted around, facing her sister fully. "That's not a very kind thing to say to the woman who just saved your feet."

Dinah laughed. "I mean it. You help anyone; you give and give. Just look at us. It's my own fault my boots are too tight. When I got measured, I told the maid I wanted my boots snug. Hearing the actual size of my feet pricked my vanity and I wanted boots to make them at least *appear* smaller." Dinah sat up. "You should tell me it's my own fault and I should wear my boots now, no matter what."

"Very well," Eliza said with a smile. "It's your own fault, and you should wear your own snug boots now, no matter what."

"But are you going to take them off, wrestle me to the ground to get yours back, and force me?"

"Of course not."

Dinah gave her a nod, as though Eliza's statement proved she was right all along, and rested back against the couch once more.

"One of these days," Dinah said, "you are going to meet a man who is perfect for you. But even if he does propose, you'll never accept him. Because you'll be too busy helping everyone else to even see it. Either that, or you'll think so highly of him, you'll want someone else to marry him."

Eliza's stomach twisted in a strange way—a manner she'd never before felt. "That doesn't even make sense."

Female voices flowed in from the corridor. It would seem the rest of the party was coming back inside.

"It's your strange, deluded mind, not mine," Dinah said, sitting up properly and smoothing her skirt.

Eliza did the same—the less proof that they'd swapped boots, the better. She truly did not want the attention. "I'm not deluded," she said in a low voice lest they be overheard. "I am thoughtful."

The door opened and all the women hurried back inside.

Still, Dinah took the moment before the women were close to lean over and whisper, "Thoughtful to a fault. Mark my words."

CHAPTER FIVE

dam sat down to dinner, Miss Kitty directly to his left. She'd refused to speak to him ever since breakfast. Over a plate of eggs and toast, he'd mentioned he expected her to work hard and apply herself to whatever her governess requested she learn. She was *his* ward, after all, and he'd only been trying to impress upon her what was expected.

Miss Kitty, apparently, didn't take well to having *anything* impressed upon her. She'd declared he wasn't her master and stomped upstairs. After he'd returned from an afternoon at White's, the governess, Miss Notley, had informed him that Miss Kitty had flatly refused to do anything she'd been told all day.

Now the young girl was sitting with her chin held high. She refused to make eye contact with him or even to speak to him. Her small rebellion was affecting the entire table, moreover. Aunt Priscilla, sitting at the foot of the table, kept shooting Adam glances, as though she expected him to say exactly the right words to change Miss Kitty's behavior. Theodosia was as quiet as usual, only now she shuffled a bit uncomfortably. Even the footmen and other members of the staff seemed to be walking on eggshells. Though Adam's father had been the owner of Lambert House, he was beginning to suspect it was actually Miss Kitty who'd been master. Earnest was the only one who didn't seem to notice the tension in the air. He ate freely, occasionally asking a question of either Adam or Aunt Priscilla.

How Earnest managed to miss the tension, Adam wasn't at all sure. But he probably hadn't been the most observant when he was fifteen either.

"Have you met any beautiful ladies yet?" Earnest asked, barely glancing up at Adam before shoving another bite of roasted vegetables into his mouth.

Aunt Priscilla tsked. "Don't be vulgar."

Earnest spoke through a mouthful. "I was only asking."

"There are many lovely ladies in London this year," Adam said. Hopefully, that would satisfy his cousin while also keeping the conversation proper. "Though I probably ought to meet more of them." He hazarded a glanced toward Miss Kitty. "A lady of the house may be exactly what Lambert House needs."

"Most certainly," Aunt Priscilla said, also casting Miss Kitty a quick look. "Lambert House has clearly gone far too long without a woman's guidance. I completely agree. The sooner you find yourself a wife, the better."

He hadn't exactly been thinking of securing himself a wife *soon*. Though he personally wished to not wed until his mourning was fully over, there was certainly nothing unseemly about a gentleman courting or even becoming engaged while still in mourning. Further still, the more he pondered on the idea, the more merit he could see in it. He was the last of the Lambert line; the sooner he married and produced an heir, the safer it would be for everyone. Miss Kitty still refused to look at him and hadn't said a word during the whole meal. However, she had perked up a bit at the talk of Adam marrying. Bringing in a woman who could see to Miss Kitty—now that sounded like a good idea.

Of course, she'd have to be a kind woman. Adam wouldn't tolerate anyone mistreating Miss Kitty. And, though he had no grandiose ideas of marrying for love, he did intend to find a woman he could respect. Someone who could tolerate his style of clothing would be a boon as well. And by "style" he truly meant wearing whatever he wanted, whenever he wanted.

If Aunt Priscilla was any indication, Adam would be hard-pressed indeed to find someone who had no opinions on his clothing. Though Theodosia didn't ever seem to care what he wore. Perhaps a woman like her would suit?

There was that woman he'd met at the ball—the one who'd inadvertently tripped him. He smiled at the memory.

"If you ask me," Aunt Priscilla said, "if ever there was a time to find a proper wife, it is now. You are new, so everyone will want to meet you. The Season has only begun, and there will be many opportunities to meet young ladies equal to your status."

It was a valid argument. If he waited eight or nine months under the excuse that he wanted to get his bearings first, the Season would be over, and there would be very few young ladies to meet. Now *was* a most opportune time to consider finding himself a wife in all seriousness.

"Of course," Aunt Priscilla spoke on without requiring a response, not for the first time, "she will need to be someone of respectable standing. Connections are everything in London."

"Yes, Aunt," he said with a small smile. He loved his aunt, but she could be quite determined to see her own will done.

"She ought to have a father who will propel your own influence upward. Elegant, poised."

"Yes, Aunt."

The dining room door opened, and Mr. Reid walked in, causing Aunt Priscilla to stop her rant. Adam still found himself staring nearly every time he saw the butler. One of these days, he truly did need to discover how Mr. Reid had come to the position at such a young age.

"Pardon me, my lord," Mr. Reid said with a bow. "Lord Honeyfield and his daughter, Lady Augusta, are requesting an audience."

Miss Kitty suddenly pushed away from the table and darted from the room.

Adam watched her go, too surprised to say anything. Mr. Reid, for his part, barely batted an eye. Adam wished he could ask the butler what it was about Lord Honeyfield's visit that made Miss Kitty feel she must leave to hide. However, though the staff respected him, he wasn't eager to show his ineptitude by asking pointless questions.

"A visit at this hour?" Aunt Priscilla asked.

Adam glanced down at his meal. He was mostly done anyway. He placed his napkin down and scooted his chair back. "Very well. Have them shown into the drawing room." Perhaps a brief visit would give him some insight into Miss Kitty.

"Very good, my lord." Mr. Reid gave another brief bow and then strode from the room.

Aunt Priscilla made to stand as well, but Adam held up a hand. "Do not trouble yourself, Aunt. I am sure it will be a brief visit."

"But he brought his daughter. Surely you two gentlemen cannot visit without another woman present to keep her company."

"We shall be fine, I assure you. I will see to it that our conversation stays most proper."

Aunt Priscilla didn't look convinced, but she remained seated. Adam strode out of the room and up the stairs. The drawing room door was open, and Miss Kitty's voice floated out. So she'd come to *see* the visitors, not to hide from them.

"He is mean and arrogant and stubborn."

Adam entered the room, and though he knew Miss Kitty saw him, she didn't stop her diatribe.

"He says I must do *everything* Miss Notley wants me to do. I can't do that many calculations." Miss Kitty sat on the lap of a young lady with hair set in perfect curls about her face.

"Good evening."

Adam turned to his right and found an older man standing not far to the side.

"Lord Honeyfield, I presume?" Adam asked.

"One and the same. Your late father and I were good friends."

"It is a pleasure to meet you." Adam tried to ignore Miss Kitty's voice, though the girl didn't stop talking. It was possible that after a day of not speaking, she simply had too many words built up inside of her to do anything but ramble.

Lord Honeyfield bowed his head. "I apologize for the late hour. I had wished to come sooner and pay my respects to you, but other business has kept me in the South until today. Please accept my deepest condolences regarding the passing of your father."

"Thank you, sir. It is very good of you to come."

Miss Kitty's voice suddenly rose. "He absolutely exhausts me!"

Lord Honeyfield coughed out a small laugh, then motioned toward the young lady. "My daughter, Lady Augusta. She and Miss Kitty have become something like close friends these past several weeks."

Lady Augusta met Adam's gaze and gave him a brief nod. But she didn't stop Miss Kitty's ever-continuing speech long enough to actually stand and curtsy. With a soft smile on her lips, Lady Augusta returned her full attention to Miss Kitty.

She was a nice enough woman to look at, he supposed. Miss Kitty clearly adored her. Had not Adam, only moments ago, been thinking he needed to find himself a wife who was kind to Miss Kitty? It was as though the heavens had opened and placed one directly in his drawing room. Now, if only he could ascertain how she felt about jackets that clashed with breeches.

"If you have a minute," Lord Honeyfield said, "I had hoped we might sit for a bit. Get to know one another a little better. I know your father always intended to be here when you arrived, help you get your footing about London and what not." His voice grew soft. "I would be honored if you'd allow me to do so in his stead."

Adam turned back toward the man. The man who possibly could help him understand who his own father had been better than anyone else alive. He seemed a good sort of fellow. And, at the moment, Adam needed all the help he could find. "The honor would be all mine."

CHAPTER SIX

One of the footmen walked silently into the drawing room and handed Eliza a note before moving back out again.

"Don't tell me you've already acquired a secret admirer," Dinah said without looking up from her embroidery.

"Oh, hush." Eliza opened the small note. It was only the two of them in the drawing room this morning, but that didn't mean Eliza wished for Dinah's constant teasing.

Eliza dear,

Lady Honeyfield wrote me to say she and her daughter would be coming to call on me this morning. If you, Rachel, and Dinah would be so kind as to join us, I would very much appreciate the company. If you cannot make it, send word. Otherwise, I shall send a carriage for you in half an hour's time.

Lady Blackmore

"Well?" Dinah asked.

"It seems we have been invited to Lady Blackmore's home."

"Again? And so soon?"

Eliza nodded, handing the note over to her sister. They'd only been at her ladyship's home two days before. Eliza didn't think any of them had fully understood just how involved the Lady Blackmore wished to be when the marchioness had first offered to help them all enter society. Between instructing them almost daily, forever introducing them to new people, and her frequent visits to discuss with Father "how to make the most" of this Season, Eliza saw Lady Blackmore enough to nearly consider the woman family.

Dinah put the note down. "I, for one, am glad. Let me finish this flower, and we can be on our way."

At least one of them was excited to be forever coming and going. Eliza stood. "I shall go tell Rachel."

They were all ready in the half-hour before the carriage arrived, aided by the fact that while their abigail did Dinah's hair, Eliza did Rachel's. Though Rachel hadn't said as much aloud, Eliza guessed by the way she'd donned her best morning dress that she was pleased by the invitation as well.

It wasn't as though Eliza herself was *displeased*. Only, she had been savoring the peaceful, slow-paced morning. Of all the niceties they'd enjoyed since Father's knighthood, time to calmly sit and relax had been Eliza's favorite. If only she could persuade Father to take her out on horseback now and then, she would be quite happy in her new situation.

They arrived at Lady Blackmore's home not five minutes before Lady Honeyfield and Lady Augusta.

While the older two women carried on a discussion with Rachel and Dinah regarding the latest fashion and what they might expect later this Season when more families arrived, Lady Augusta drew Eliza aside.

"I am going to risk our new friendship," Lady Augusta said in a soft voice even while sitting down atop a window bench, "and admit I willingly listened in on some gossip yesterday."

"Very well." Eliza sat beside her, the rainy day providing little in the way of light. At least it wasn't snowing.

"It was regarding your family."

"Now I'm more wary than anything."

"Tell me it's true," Lady Augusta said, placing a hand on Eliza's arm. "I would dearly love to believe that it's true, that is. So tell me, did your father truly stop highwaymen from killing our sweet Lady

Blackmore? Did he step between her and their guns and boldly declare they wouldn't hurt her?"

Eliza laughed. "Well, it didn't happen *quite* like that." Despite her father's insistence she stay well away, Eliza had slipped up close and seen everything herself. It wasn't as though she was going to sit back among the trees wondering if she was ever going to see her father again.

"But there were highwaymen threatening her, right?"

"Yes, but only three."

"Did he actually step directly in the line of fire?"

It was strange to talk about the day that had so terrified her with someone who only saw it as a heroic deed. Still, she could understand Lady Augusta's awe. She felt the same way whenever she thought back to that day. "He actually shot two of them before they could pull their guns on him. One in the shoulder and the other in the thigh. Both injuries bled too much for the men to use their weapons after that. Then my father hit the third over the head with his rifle. Knocked him unconscious with one blow."

"Dear me." Lady Augusta lifted a hand to her throat.

"Are you all right?" Eliza asked. Her friend had suddenly gone a bit pale.

Lady Augusta slowly shut her eyes and shook her head. "I guess I've never heard such . . . detailed descriptions before."

Eliza snapped her mouth shut. "Forgive me. I forget my place."

"It is quite all right." Lady Augusta smiled, though it appeared somewhat forced.

No, it wasn't all right. Eliza ought to have remembered that here, among the gentle ladies of society, one never spoke of blood or of being knocked unconscious.

"I am in earnest," Lady Augusta said, her voice returning to its usual strength. "And if you think I'm one of those silly, shallow ladies who's going to dismiss you out of hand for speaking differently when you were raised differently—well, you don't know me well enough." She sat up straighter, once more her normal color. "We're friends, and you can't convince me that we are otherwise."

Eliza smiled. "I'm glad to hear that. I hadn't thought to make many friends here in London." Having at least one would make life much easier.

"And now that I understand where you're coming from," Lady Augusta said, "I better see why you were so hesitant to meet gentlemen at the ball the other night."

"Was it so obvious?" Eliza had rather hoped no one but her family and Lady Blackmore had realized her reluctance.

"I'm afraid so," Lady Augusta said, twisting her lips to the side. She sat up fully and turned toward Eliza. "I just had a brilliant idea."

Eliza had no notion what it might be.

"I shall take you under my wing," Lady Augusta declared. "I will help you find your footing in society. We shall be thick as thieves and clever as foxes. You'll have your husband by the end of the Season, or my name isn't Augusta."

"Oh," Eliza said, willing herself not to visibly shrink away from the notion. "I don't think that's at all necessary. I am sure between Lady Blackmore's connections and—"

"Of course she has ever so many connections, but connections won't be enough. My sister Jane has told me everything one needs to know about a London Season. No, connections will not be enough. We need you to draw *attention*."

That was exactly what Eliza was trying to avoid. "No, seriously—"

"We'll dress you up more elegantly than anything the peerage has ever seen before. You'll have flocks of gentlemen vying for your hand."

"I'm pretty sure one will be enough."

"Hush now, I'm planning. We'll start with showing you off at my mother's card party the day after tomorrow. You have no other obligations this afternoon, correct?"

"We are at Lady Blackmore's disposal."

"I'm certain she'll allow you to stay. We'll spend the day studying everything Jane ever wrote to me about catching a man's eye. Come the card party, you shall be ready."

A full afternoon deep in discussion regarding furtive glances, flirtatious waves of one's fan, and coquettish eyelash batting was more than enough to make Eliza want to sink into a hole and never come out again. Not once, not a single time all afternoon at Lady Honeyfield's home, could Eliza do any of the things Augusta had asked her to do without blushing furiously.

Augusta promptly, though kindly, informed her that she blushed far too much to be considered stylish and asked if she could please bring it down a bit. Of course Eliza couldn't. She wasn't blushing for her own amusement. Their discussion regarding her red face lasted over half an hour.

Eliza stepped down from the carriage Lady Honeyfield had been so kind as to summon to take her home. She'd stayed long enough that Augusta had insisted she eat dinner with her family. It had been a friendly, talkative meal. By the end, Lady Honeyfield had even seemed to warm to Eliza, if only slightly. Still, it had been one meal Eliza could have done without. After so much time trying to be something she felt certain she would never fully become, she was ready for some time alone. Eliza hugged her pelisse close as the carriage rattled off and into the night. At least she was home now. And here in London, the house Father was letting had enough rooms that each of them had their own bedchamber. It was a luxury that Eliza still reveled in nightly.

"Miss Mulgrave?" A deep man's voice came from her right. "Is that really you?"

She turned and found a soldier in full uniform studying her closely. He seemed familiar—something about the nose and cheekbones. Three other soldiers stood just behind him, watching them silently.

"It is you." He smiled and walked up to her. "What are the chances we'd met again here in London, of all places?"

As he approached, candlelight from the porch fell more fully across his features.

"Mr. Collin?"

He gave her a formal bow. "One and the same."

"I can believe it—what I don't believe is that you're here." Last she'd heard, he'd been sent to the continent. She half expected one of these days to learn that he'd died there, either in battle or later from his wounds, as so many had.

He laughed loud enough that it echoed harshly against the houses on either side of the road. There was a smell of drink about him. She didn't remember him being partial to drink in the past.

"Whatever are you doing here?" she asked, glancing behind him at his fellow soldiers.

Mr. Collin shrugged, motioning toward the men. "We were"—his gaze jumped to the side as he shifted about—"just out enjoying the night air."

Something in his jovial tone rang untrue. "Is that all?" She tried to keep her question light.

"Never mind me." He waved off her question. "What are you doing here?"

Of course she shouldn't be prying into his affairs. They had known one another at one time, but that was many years ago. They were barely more than acquaintances now. "That is a very long story."

"Don't tell me this is your home?" he asked, motioning toward the townhouse.

She looked over at it—it certainly was far nicer than anything she had ever dreamed she might live in. "It is. Surprising, isn't it?"

"Certainly." His voice held awe. Then he came to himself. "Not that I ever believed you deserved less."

He always had been very kind to her.

"You don't live here"—his brow dropped—"with your husband, do you?"

"Oh, gracious no," Eliza said with a laugh. "My father is letting the house for the Season."

"Here for a proper London Season, are you now?"

Eliza curtsied. "That I am."

"Well, well. I think I need to hear that long story you mentioned." He glanced over his shoulder at the other soldiers.

Though they were waiting silently, Eliza got the impression they were eager to be on their way.

"Suppose," Mr. Collin said, "I call on you some morning? Perhaps the day after tomorrow?"

A heat as familiar as it was unwanted burned against Eliza's cheeks. What was it Augusta had told her that afternoon? *Suck in your stomach and tell yourself you're far and above any of this. It always helps my blushes go away.*

Eliza tried, but she didn't feel better for any of it. At least in the dark, Mr. Collin probably wouldn't see her red face too clearly.

"That would be lovely," she said.

"Excellent." Mr. Collin's smile grew, and he bowed once more. "Until then."

Eliza smiled back. "Until then."

CHAPTER SEVEN

E liza placed both reins in her left hand and tipped her head back. The sun shone brightly this morning, though the clouds on the horizon promised it wouldn't last long.

"It is nice to get out, is it not?" Father asked, astride Brushfire.

Eliza breathed in the air deeply. It was not at all the same air that she was used to, but at least they were outside, and there were no judgmental stares to hamper her mood. At this time in the morning, Hyde Park was, quite blessedly, empty.

"Heavenly," she said. "Though I cannot wonder that you dare leave the house before your morning tête-à-tête with Lady Blackmore."

Father didn't laugh at the tease, but his lips ticked up to the side and he let out a grunt. "No doubt she'll be waiting for me when we return, full of some new idea on how to show you three girls off in the best light possible."

"Will she wait, though?" It had been ages since she and Father had taken a ride together, and she rather suspected he was hoping for as long a ride as she was.

"That woman could out-wait a famine," he muttered.

Once more they fell into a comfortable silence and wordlessly

63

enjoyed the gentle rock of the horses beneath them. They rode around Hyde Park a few more times. Eliza adored her time with Father, especially when it included riding Starfire. But it rarely included much conversation.

A gentleman riding a completely black horse turned into the park. He was too far away for Eliza to see anything other than that his jacket was a heinous yellow-green color and he had a rather fine seat. Instead of turning his back toward them, however, the gentleman faced his horse in their direction and started riding their way.

Oh, and she recognized him, too. It was the same man she'd met at the ball only a week and a half ago.

"Tell me," she asked Father, "have you formed many acquaintances at White's?" Lady Blackmore had seen to it that he received admittance to the club and the exclusive society therein. Father had proudly professed no need for such favors for over three days before finally capitulating.

"A few, I suppose," he grumbled. "Mostly the place is full of nonsense."

Though Father would probably never admit as much, Eliza suspected he actually found himself enjoying White's. He'd gone a second time, after all.

"How about the gentleman riding toward us?" She hoped Father knew him. Eliza couldn't very well ignore him, but neither could she address him since she didn't know who he was. Botheration, but this was the exact type of situation she wasn't the least bit knowledgeable of how to handle.

Father studied the rider drawing ever closer but didn't give her any indication if he was familiar with the gentleman or not. Another minute and he was too close for them to speak without being overheard.

The gentleman pulled his horse to a halt beside them. "Good morning to you both."

Eliza inclined her head as did her father.

"Good morning, Lord Lambert," Father said.

So he did know the man, and he was a lord, at that; Eliza sat up a bit straighter. Lord Lambert looked her way, a smile brightening his face. She'd begun to wonder if she hadn't started to dream him up as more handsome than he actually was—but no. He was every bit as beautiful as she remembered—something she'd done more than she ought since their chance meeting.

"Have you met my daughter?" Father asked, though the words were a bit drawn out as though he didn't actually wish them spoken.

"We have not been introduced," Lord Lambert said.

The way he spoke the truth without admitting to their less-than-proper conversation from before made Eliza smile.

"This is my eldest daughter, Miss Mulgrave."

It was strange hearing Father call her by such a formal name. He'd always introduced her as Eliza before he'd been knighted, no matter who they'd been speaking with at the time. It made her a touch sad to simply be called "Miss Mulgrave"—it seemed to place a distance between her and whomever she spoke with.

"Eliza," Father continued, "This is Lord Lambert."

Sitting atop their horses, both she and Lord Lambert simply inclined their heads toward one another.

"It is a pleasure to meet you, Miss Mulgrave."

"And I, you," she said.

Father's gaze had moved off toward the other side of the park; apparently, it was up to her to keep the conversation going or bring it to an end.

"Would you care to ride with us for a bit?" she asked. Since Father had not expressed that he wished for Lord Lambert to leave them be, Eliza sincerely hoped it was all right if she prolonged their time together.

"That sounds quite pleasant, indeed," Lord Lambert said, turning his horse about so it faced the same direction as Starfire.

Eliza glanced over at Father. He didn't say anything, only urged his horse forward.

"You have quite a lovely mare," Lord Lambert said as they fell in behind Father, riding at a speed that allowed for easy conversation.

"Father gave her to me when she was only a foal. I named her Starfire."

"A fine name for a fine horse."

"And what of your mount, my lord?" Eliza asked. "He looks to be quite a powerful steed."

"That he is." Lord Lambert's voice was filled with evident pride. "I, too, received him when he was only a colt."

"His coloring is most striking." It wasn't often a horse was *entirely* black. There seemed not to be a single marking on his entire coat.

"Striking, and the inspiration behind his own name: Black Beard."

Eliza laughed. "A beautiful horse like him, and the most inspiring name you could come up with was 'Black Beard'?"

Lord Lambert tried to appear affronted, but it was clearly more an act than true hurt. "I was but a boy at the time, you will realize. In my young mind, Black Beard was quite an awe-inspiring name."

"Come now." Eliza eyed the horse more closely. "He can't be more than ten years old. Twelve at the oldest, I'd say."

Lord Lambert's eyebrow ticked up. "You know horses quite well. I'm impressed."

Eliza tried to ignore the warmth his compliment brought to her cheeks.

"You are right," he continued. "Black Beard will be eleven in a few months."

"Knowing that, then, do you still profess to have only been a boy when you got him?"

He chuckled. "Very well, you have caught me. I was fourteen at the time. But to a fourteen-year-old lad, Black Beard sounded very awe-inspiring."

"I shall have to take your word for it."

"Have you no brothers?"

Eliza shook her head. "Only a sister and a cousin who is more sister than distant relative, since she's lived with us for almost eight years now."

"Pity that. I understand most ladies enjoy having a brother around to tease them," he said, waggling his eyebrows.

"Is that your take on it?"

"It is, and I defy you to change my mind."

Eliza laughed. It seemed Lady Blackmore was more correct in her decree that Eliza could find friends here in London than she'd realized. There would always be snide remarks and those who looked down on her, but here was a second individual who put her at her ease and helped her smile. Perhaps London wouldn't be all bad after all.

"Regardless of your personal feelings on the subject," she began, "foolish though they may be—"

"Foolish?"

Eliza smiled more. "I still profess there is nothing for you to pity. Just think, if my father had had a son, he probably would not have taught *me* so much about horses."

Lord Lambert donned the look of a wise man, solemnly agreeing. "That would have been an egregious travesty indeed."

Adam dismounted and allowed the manservant to lead Black Beard away. It was far later in the day than he'd originally planned on returning to Lambert House. But he hadn't wanted to stop his conversation with Miss Mulgrave. The first few drops of rain hit against his cheek and hands. Hopefully, Miss Mulgrave and her father had been able to reach their home by now. If the darkness of the clouds was any indicator, they were going to open and really pour any minute.

Mr. Reid opened the front door for Adam as he hurried in. "Pleasant ride, my lord?"

Adam handed him his hat and greatcoat. "Very pleasant, thank you."

There was a crash from a few floors up and what sounded like Miss Kitty's angry voice.

"She's in a state again this morning," Mr. Reid said, looking toward the top of the stairs.

Adam followed his gaze. "Was she often like this before my father passed?"

Mr. Reid gave him a puzzled expression. "Of course not, my lord. Never." Adam got the distinct impression Mr. Reid believed Adam should already know as much.

"She was always a peaceful, lovable girl," Mr. Reid continued. "Begging your pardon, though, I believe she's taken his death far harder than the rest of us." He rocked his head back and forth. "Seems only fitting, though, seeing as she knew him better than all of us."

She'd known his father well, then? Mr. Reid hurried off, but Adam remained rooted to the spot. He had a distinct vision of his father growing up. He had always envisioned a man who looked quite a bit like himself, only with wrinkles and white hair; a man sitting behind a grand desk, with papers organized in stacks around him, and prominent gentlemen sitting across from him; a man who was fair, but firm.

And, on the whole, the things he'd learned from Lord Honeyfield regarding his father matched that idea. Lord Honeyfield had spoken of their times at White's, the late Lord Lambert's views on Parliament, and even his thoughts on the war with France.

Only, those weren't the only things Adam was learning about his father. There were other pieces of information, things that didn't come from Lord Honeyfield, nor society in general. And none of which seemed to mesh with what he'd always thought of the man.

Apparently, Father had passed after acquiring a ward. Did that make him a man with a mistress?

Not only that, but he apparently spent a great deal of time with the young girl. Now, the image of a fair but firm gentleman sitting behind the grand desk morphed to include him sitting at a child's table, sipping tea out of a play cup, dolls sitting to either side of him.

Whomever his father had been, he had also been a man who visited his only son no more than a couple of times in twenty years. And yet, he had cared so extensively for this young girl?

Adam shook his head. He couldn't seem to reconcile the differing accounts of his father's character.

Regardless, there was a young girl upstairs who had known his father quite well. Might she be willing to speak of the late Lord Lambert as freely as Lord Honeyfield had been? Perhaps, if he learned more, the blurred image Adam now carried of his father would eventually calm and become clear.

Adam took the stairs quickly, hurrying up flight after flight. The townhouse was narrow; what it lacked in width, it made up for in height. Unfortunately, that meant climbing several sets of stairs several times a day.

The nursery was on the top floor. The door stood open, and Miss Notley's voice floated out.

"Yes, Miss Kitty, you must clean up the mess. It is of your own making."

"No!" Miss Kitty yelled. "I won't!"

The governess's age was somewhere between Adam's and Aunt Priscilla's, if he had to guess. She'd shown herself to be a very level-headed woman who provided a calming effect on Miss Kitty. However, it seemed this morning even that was not enough.

Adam reached the door. The room was quite a sight. A small table had been tipped on its side, chairs scattered around it, and not one upright. Papers littered the floor. There was a doll in the center of the room, lying on her back.

Standing close to the window was the mess-maker herself. She stood with half her curls pulled back with a nice ribbon and the other half dangling at odd angles around her face. Her face was screwed up tight, and her fists were placed against her hips.

Adam stepped into the room. "Perhaps, Miss Notley, you would care for a break just now."

"I am quite all right, my lord." It was to her credit that her voice didn't show any signs of distress. Always collected, she most certainly was.

"Still," Adam said, "I would like a moment with Miss Kitty."

"Very well, my lord." She curtsied and then slipped out of the room.

Miss Kitty watched him, openly wary.

Now that he was alone with the girl, Adam suddenly wasn't sure how to begin. "Shall we sit?" he asked.

Miss Kitty nodded but didn't say anything. She righted first one of the small, toppled chairs and then a second, which she sat in.

"Lambert always sat in that one," she said, pointing to the first chair.

She'd called his father "Lambert," not "*Lord* Lambert," not "his lordship." Their relationship must have been a close one. Adam strode over to the chair and lowered himself carefully onto it. This young girl referred to his father the same way another gentleman at White's would have. Another small insight that messed with the image of his father he'd always had.

With his knees sticking up ridiculously high, Adam faced the girl.

"Well?" she asked. "You wished to speak to me?"

"Yes."

She turned her face away from him before he could respond. "I don't care what you have to say, I'm not cleaning this room."

"Yes, Miss Kitty, you will need to clean this room." He wasn't about to let her off so easily. "However, I have actually come to speak about something else. Perhaps we can postpone cleaning until we have had our chat?"

She glanced back over at him, her lips pursed tight. "Very well."

He wasn't sure if Miss Kitty realized she'd just agreed to clean up, after all; either way, he did wish to ask her a few questions first. "I understand you knew my father."

"Lambert?"

There it was again—that familiarity. Far more than Adam could boast. "Yes. I wondered if you might tell me about him."

Her brow creased. "He died," she said flatly.

Adam chuckled. "I know that much. I meant, I wondered if you would tell me what you knew about him."

The question seemed to only confuse her more. Perhaps it was too ambiguous for such a young girl.

"Tell me," Adam tried instead, "what you two used to do together."

Apparently, he'd finally stumbled upon the right words. For the next hour, Miss Kitty spoke of taking tea and showing off her drawings, of reciting French verbs, and even sitting on his lap while he read stories aloud.

Adam remained silent most of the time, only inserting a little *hmm* or a *tell me more* here and there to let her know he was truly listening. She certainly painted a very different picture than the one Adam had always envisioned. The few times his father had visited, he'd been stern, aloof. He certainly hadn't read Adam any stories. All the letters he had written to Adam had spoken of how busy he'd been, how preoccupied he had been with matters of estate business and Parliament. Yet, he'd found time for Miss Kitty? It left Adam confused, and, if he was being honest, a bit hurt.

"We went to the menagerie last year," Miss Kitty said. "I saw a tiger. Lambert said the tiger was a kitty like I am a Kitty. Do you think I'd make a good tiger?"

"The best," Adam said.

"But I don't particularly care for the color orange."

"You like blue better?" he asked, pointing toward the single blue ribbon in her hair.

"This is my prettiest ribbon. But I like purple, too. Have you gotten me more ribbons for my hair yet?"

Ah, blast. He'd forgotten about that promise. He wasn't used to having a little girl to watch over. "Not yet, but I will. Soon."

"Maybe you can get me some purple?"

"I'll keep my eyes open for some, Miss Kitty."

"Lambert always called me Kitty, not Miss."

"Would you like me to do the same?"

She watched him for a bit then nodded once. "But I can't call you Lambert. You're not your father."

Truer words had never been spoken. "Very well. What would you like to call me?"

"Do you have another name?"

He'd grown up being called Lord Robins, and sometimes he missed the courtesy title, but he couldn't ask her to call him that. "You may call me Adam. Will that work?"

"That's a very fine name," she said, standing. She walked over to him and patted his arm, almost maternally. Had she learned the act from his father? "I can tell you about your father again sometime."

"And I'll bring you ribbons for your hair."

She smiled brightly. "I think I like you, after all, Adam."

"And I like you, Kitty."

CHAPTER EIGHT

The morning Eliza expected Mr. Collin to call, she encouraged Rachel and Dinah to visit some of the shops while she stayed at home. She hadn't mentioned Mr. Collin to anyone. Not even Father. She wasn't sure why she'd kept their meeting a secret; it wasn't as though anything untoward had happened. Only, every time she opened her mouth to say something, she found that words escaped her, and she simply remained silent.

The door to the drawing room opened and a footman entered. "Mr. Collin to see you, miss."

So he'd finally come. Her stomach clenched. It had occurred to her several times these past couple of days that he very well might not be the same man she remembered. She hadn't known him well to begin with, and now years of life and experience stood between them.

Mr. Collin strode into the room. He was in uniform again, the rich dark blue fabric and gold buttons looking formal and almost regal.

"Good morning," he said with a bright smile.

"Good morning. Would you care to sit?" She motioned toward the settee across from the chair she occupied.

"Thank you, yes."

How strange to converse so formally with someone she'd known so many years ago, well before he was dressed in uniform and she was the daughter of a knight.

They sat, silent. Finally, Eliza opened her mouth to say, "How have you fared these past years?" only to hear him speak at the same moment, "I had not expected to see you in London."

She let out a nervous laugh, even as Mr. Collin sat back. "Please excuse me. Ladies first."

"I wanted to ask how you've fared these past years."

"It has been quite a while since last we saw one another, hasn't it?"

"Indeed." The drawing room door opened, and a maid bustled in, a large tea tray in her hands. "But I would dearly love to hear all about it."

"I'll talk if you pour. One thing a man learns fast aboard a ship, the next cup of decent tea is never a guarantee."

Eliza poured as he spoke, seeing that a few pieces of cake were added to his plate as well.

"I have been well. The Navy has been a good home. I was made boatswain early last year and have quite enjoyed the new challenge."

"That is impressive." She offered the tea and cake out to him. "Though, I admit, it came as rather a surprise to me that you joined the Navy at all."

Mr. Collin leaned back, sipping at the tea. "It was as much a surprise to myself as it was to you. But, I don't suppose it stayed a secret forever that my family fell on unexpected hard times. Still, it was not easy joining the Navy at the age I did. Most join as boys, closer to twelve than sixteen."

"But if you've been made boatswain, you can't have struggled too much."

He downed the rest of his tea in one swallow. "I made a few friends, and they helped me find my sea legs, both on the ocean and off."

She could certainly relate to finding herself in a whole new world, one she had never expected to be in. "Friends can be most important in finding one's sea legs, I have learned." She picked up one of the small slices of cake—it was far lighter than anything she'd ever enjoyed before coming to Town. Life could certainly change in an instant. "Do you refer to the men you were with the other night?"

"Oh, no, they are just a few men I happened to meet here in London. My ship currently patrols the southern border. I am only here for a few weeks. On holiday, you might say. But tell me how *you* came to be here."

"It is quite a story." One she'd had much practice telling.

"Pour me another cup, and I shall listen to the whole thing without interrupting once."

Eliza stepped into Lord and Lady Honeyfield's grand home beside Dinah, Rachel, and Lady Blackmore. Father had chosen not to join them. Unlike the townhouse Father was letting, this home abutted no others to either side. The cottage Eliza used to live in could have easily fit four times over inside this spacious home. She'd been too overwhelmed with Augusta's plans to really appreciate the splendor of their home the first time she'd visited. But now, arriving with her whole family and Lady Blackmore as expected guests for dinner and cards, Eliza felt wholly insignificant. Fresh flowers covered every side table in the entryway and a grand coat of arms lined one wall. Soon, a footman took their things, and they were shown into the parlor room off to their right. Already, several guests were present. There were a couple of matrons Eliza recognized from the ball a few weeks back. But most of the individuals present were strangers to her. Though it was still too early in the spring to be warm, Eliza felt the house was far too hot for her liking. The hair along the back of her neck stuck to her skin and she struggled to breathe deeply.

"Hello, my dear." Augusta hurried over to Eliza and took hold of her hands. Leaning in, she pressed her cheek next to Eliza's, taking the opportunity to whisper, "Do you remember all we discussed?"

Eliza nodded. "But I don't think we covered how to avoid fainting in nearly enough detail."

"You shall be brilliant. Just you wait and see."

Arm in arm, they walked about the room. Augusta introduced Eliza to first one and then a second gentleman. Eliza tried her best to do all her friend had instructed her. She smiled, but not too big; she agreed with the men, but not too emphatically; she brought up acceptable topics when the conversation lagged and even managed to keep her blushing to a minimum. She did well enough, Eliza believed, but heavens, it took a lot of effort. So much so, she felt nigh on ready to collapse by the time dinner was announced.

"Do forgive us for being so late." A refined woman of indeterminate years hurried into the room, loudly greeting Lady Honeyfield. "Only my nephew"—she turned, apparently expecting said nephew to be directly behind her, only to find no one there—"I say, isn't that so like a bachelor? One minute here, the next gone."

Just then, Lord Lambert walked into the room, his attire even more singular than when he'd happened upon Eliza and her father the other day. This time, instead of an off-putting green jacket, he'd donned a plum-colored one, the black band still present around his arm. On its own, the jacket wasn't overly hideous, only it clashed most abominably with his brown breeches.

"Come and greet our hostess," his aunt said, waving him closer.

As he strode further into the room, his eye caught Eliza's, and he smiled. Eliza smiled back—her first sincere smile of the night. Another friend she could count on to not judge her or look down at her. It was a welcome sight. He turned away from her when he reached his aunt and Lady Honeyfield. The three of them quickly fell into a soft conversation.

"It appears we have been granted a couple more minutes to talk before having to go into dinner," Augusta said to her and the two gentlemen they spoke with. "How shall we fill it?"

"For my part," said Lord Down, the taller of the two gentlemen, "I should like to hear how Miss Mulgrave finds London." He turned toward her, his nose lifting. "No doubt, we have quite put you in awe."

Eliza felt her stomach tighten. There was no warmth in his tone, only lofty superiority.

"I find London to my liking." That was what people said, wasn't it?

"Well, I don't," Mr. Fitzroy, the shorter of the two, said. "There never seems to be the right amount of people. Not enough now, then, overnight, too many. Then it's too hot, and soon after, far too cold. No, give me the country, I say, where there's room to have as many or as few guests over as one likes."

"Rubbish," said Down. "The country is nothing but one long bore."

Augusta shook her head. "Come, Lord Down, we cannot all love London as much as you and I. The country has many things of which to boast, does it not, Eliza?"

"Yes, most certainly." Eliza hurried to agree with her friend.

Lord Down only scoffed, eying Eliza as he muttered, "Only to those who don't know of which they speak."

Eliza felt the insult like a slender pin being stuck in her chest. If Dinah had been there, she probably would have had some witty rejoinder or smart remark. But Eliza's mind was blank.

Then it was too late, for the moment to respond had passed.

"So, tell me, Mr. Fitzroy," Augusta said, smoothly redirecting the conversation, "if you were home in the country tonight, how many people would you invite? Do tell me, are you in the mood for a small gathering or a large crush?"

Far from appearing pleased, Mr. Fitzroy's expression only looked more sour. "Lady Augusta, I could not say, for this isn't the country, and I don't know how I'd be feeling if I were there."

Blessedly, at that moment, Lord Lambert strode over to them. "Good evening."

Eliza curtsied, as did Augusta, even while the two gentlemen bowed. Greetings were exchanged, though Eliza couldn't help but wish there had been a couple of men who would avail themselves of the opportunity to take their leave. Lord Down and Mr. Fitzroy may have families all of high-standing, but for Eliza, that only meant they could look down on her from higher up.

She wouldn't let it bother her, however. It was as Lady Black-more said. There were good people everywhere. There were also pompous idiots everywhere. That didn't mean she couldn't find her way among London society.

Eliza turned toward Lord Lambert. "How was the rest of your ride the other day?"

"Quite invigorating."

"I am glad to hear it."

Augusta spoke up. "Are you rather partial to horses, Lord Lambert?"

"I am, almost as much as Miss Mulgrave."

"I should hope, as a gentleman," Lord Down said, "you are not partial to horses in the *same way* as a lady."

Lord Lambert's brow dropped. "I cannot confess to knowing what you mean."

Lord Down shook his head. "Come now. It is a well-known fact that a lady only finds horses interesting as a way to appeal to us men who naturally find them so."

Eliza's face burned.

"Thank you all for your patience," Lady Honeyfield called to all the room. "I appreciate you allowing me time to catch up with an old friend."

"Not *that* old," Lord Lambert's aunt said.

Lady Honeyfield laughed softly and Eliza tried to commit the sound to memory. It had been quite soft, not shrill, not overly titter-y. It was a perfectly ladylike sound. Eliza would have to practice it later.

"Now," Lady Honeyfield continued, "we are ready to go into dinner."

Eliza turned back to their small group, her nerves on edge. She'd worried about this moment quite a lot since they'd been issued the invitation. What kind of a gentleman offered to walk in with a woman of very low standing? Still, with there being three gentlemen standing beside only herself and Augusta, the chances that one of them would ask her to walk in with him were high. That, at least, was providential.

If only it would be Lord Lambert who asked her; he would be pleasant company as they ate. She turned slightly toward him only to see him extend his elbow toward Augusta.

A tinge of wistfulness brushed over her, but Eliza pushed it away. She was happy her friend, at least, would be seated by a good conversationalist. Nonetheless, Eliza didn't dare look over at either of the other two gentlemen. Suppose they both walked away and found other ladies? What did one do in a situation such as that? She very well couldn't walk into dinner alone.

"Miss Mulgrave?" Lord Down stretched an arm toward her. "Would you do me the honor?"

Eliza was momentarily too surprised to do or say anything. Had he not made his dislike of her known quite clearly only moments before? And the look in his eye . . . she couldn't quite make sense of it. Was he remorseful? Did he pity her?

"I thank you," she said, taking his arm. "I would be delighted." At least she and Augusta had practiced accepting such invitations.

Augusta gave Eliza a quiet smile, as though expressing her delight at seeing Lord Down ask to take Eliza into dinner. Eliza, for her part, couldn't quite find the same enthusiasm.

Unfortunately, placing a fist in another man's face over port was generally considered poor form. Not that Adam's father had ever expressly told him as much—Adam could count on one hand the number of things his father had expressly told him—yet here he was, not placing a fist in Lord Down's face despite the growing desire.

"She doesn't even know who Lord and Lady Wilton are!" Down said loudly from across the table. If the man spoke any louder, the ladies would hear him from the drawing room. "How can *anyone* not know Lord Wilton?"

"All three out at once, too," Fitzroy said, shaking his head. "Makes a man feel rather drowned."

Down laughed. "I wonder if the Mulgraves just don't know how gauche that is, or if they simply don't care."

"Or," Fitzroy said between two large sips, "they're all wanting to get husbands before society finds out how ill-suited they are."

"No doubt," Down agreed.

Adam leaned forward, ready to object. But Lord Honeyfield stood at that same moment.

"Are we ready to join the ladies?" he asked.

The rest of the men agreed. Down and Fitzroy stood and left the room without so much as glancing Adam's way. Pompous idiots, the both of them. Adam was the last to leave the dining room. With any luck, Miss Mulgrave and her sisters had enjoyed a far more pleasant time since dinner had ended than he had.

But when Adam entered the drawing room, he found Miss Mulgrave sitting atop a small chair, pushed quite close to the wall and well away from everyone else. Her head was bent low, so he could not see her face, but if he read her posture correctly, she was about done in. Adam paused only a few feet into the room. Lady Augusta was near the piano, playing cards with three other women, Miss Dinah among them. He'd come tonight expressly for the purpose of furthering his acquaintance with Lady Augusta. Between seeing how attached Kitty was to the lady and having quickly become quite good friends with Lord Honeyfield, Adam felt certain a connection between them would be well received. Still, he hated the idea of leaving Miss Mulgrave alone when she appeared in desperate need of a friend.

Lady Augusta would have to wait. Adam turned on his heel and made his way straight for Miss Mulgrave. Besides, he'd already spent most of dinner in pleasant discussion with Lady Augusta. Surely that was enough for one night.

Adam moved a chair up beside Miss Mulgrave and sat in it.

She didn't look up or even glance in his direction.

Now that he was here, sitting beside her, he suddenly realized he wasn't sure what to say. He'd rather hoped that she'd be the first to speak. Since that wasn't going to be the case, however, it was apparently up to him.

Adam searched his mind, but the only thing he could come up with was, "You are right."

Distraught though she obviously was, Miss Mulgrave's curiosity won out, and she looked over at him. "About what?"

"About sitting here." He leaned back, folding his arms. "This is a grand vantage point."

She looked back down at her lap. "I didn't sit here for the view."

"Did you not? Well, then you unknowingly stumbled upon something rather fine. Look there." He pointed toward Fitzroy. "Have you ever seen such specimen? I hear the Gloomy Goose is rather hard to find this time of year."

The corner of her lips ticked up.

"Even more so," he pressed on, "is the Disdainful Deer." When she glanced his way, he nodded toward Down.

Miss Mulgrave sat up more fully. "In my brief experience, I've found Disdainful Deer aplenty."

He had been worried such might have been the case. "I am sorry to hear it."

She shook her head, her voice dropping in volume. "I knew coming to London would not be easy."

"It is still rather a different thing knowing it will be hard and dealing with it head-on, is it not?"

"Indeed."

On that, they could relate. His time in London hadn't gone exactly as he'd expected either. "Do you know what I found waiting for me when I arrived in Town?"

She shook her head.

"A ward."

Her eyes grew wide. "You cannot be serious."

"Ah, but I am. A young girl, by the name of Miss Kitty. My father was caring for her, and now that responsibility has fallen to me."

"Well." Miss Mulgrave leaned back in her seat, her smile coming in earnest. "That does make my difficulties seem a little less unbearable."

"Glad I could be of some service."

"Next time I am tempted to fret over my predicament, I shall simply remember yours and be relieved."

He chuckled. "I felt it the least I could do, considering we are friends."

Her smile spread until her eyes lit up. "I am glad to know you consider us friends. You and Lady Augusta are the only two friends I have in London. And that, even after foolishly allowing you to know I am fond of horses."

"I've heard Down say some idiotic things in the past, but that one was a real bounder."

"I suppose I should feel honored that he should choose me to bestow such a ridiculous flout." She immediately slapped a hand over her mouth.

Adam tried to suppress his laugh, he truly did, but he'd never heard a lady use cant before.

"You must forgive me," Miss Mulgrave said, shutting her eyes and grimacing. "It is as everyone keeps saying when they think I cannot hear—I still smell of the shop."

Adam laughed harder. Her honesty was refreshing.

Miss Mulgrave pursed her lips and folded her arms. "Now you are making me wonder if we truly are friends."

"It is only you are so diverting."

"Diverting like a witty lady, or diverting like a cow who's caught his hoof in the mud?"

"The first," he said, finally regaining his composure. "Certainly the first."

"I am pleased to hear that. Only, now you have garnered quite a bit of attention from the room."

Adam glanced out toward the rest of the drawing room. Sure enough, several individuals were glancing in their direction, curiosity clearly evident in some of their expressions, disapproval evident in others.

"Never mind them," Adam said. "Let them wonder what was so delightful about our conversation."

"That is simple enough for you," Miss Mulgrave said, pointedly not facing the room. "You are not at their mercy."

"There you are wrong," he said with a smile—he wasn't about to let her slip back into her blue-devilment. "In London, *everyone* is at society's mercy."

Her voice dropped yet lower, and she spoke through gritted teeth. "Then why the *blazes* do people do this to themselves every year?"

Adam couldn't help but laugh again.

"Please stop that," Miss Mulgrave said.

"You cannot seriously say something like that and then blame *me* for finding it—"

"Diverting?" she asked, not at all sounding like she believed it herself.

He nodded. No matter what she believed, he liked that she wasn't all false modesty.

"I beg your forgiveness—again." She sat up straight, placing her hands demurely in her lap. "I shall endeavor to speak in a manner more befitting a lady."

"Please don't." He placed a hand atop hers. Even with them both wearing gloves, the touch warmed him. Her fingers seemed to curl in toward his, almost of their own accord. He wrapped his hand more completely around hers. "No matter where you find yourself, in the countryside or a London drawing room, you should always be *you.*"

"And what of the Disdainful Deer in the world?"

He shrugged. "Hunting season has to come eventually, right?"

CHAPTER NINE

"Now," said Dinah as she slumped yet further down on the settee, "if only we could get Lord Lambert to come to *all* our at-homes, Rachel and I wouldn't have to carry most of the conversation on our own."

Eliza shot her younger sister a scowl. "I'm sure I don't know what you mean."

"Don't pretend you don't know what we're talking about." Rachel shook her head, dark curls bouncing.

Eliza felt her cheeks heat, but she clamped down on the feeling. "I'm quite sure I don't."

Dinah and Rachel shared a look.

"Well, I don't," Eliza insisted. "If I did talk more tonight than usual, it was only because Augusta was here."

"You mean," Dinah said, a breathless quality to her tone, "because Augusta *brought* Lord Lambert."

"Precisely—oh, no, I meant"—Eliza cringed—"my friends were there, and I simply feel more comfortable speaking with them than I do with new acquaintances."

"And what of Mr. Collin?" Rachel asked, all fake innocence. "Is he not your friend as well? Yet you don't have half so much to say when he is present."

Eliza wished she could disagree but found she couldn't. At the end of his first visit, Mr. Collin had requested he be permitted to call again the following week. Eliza very well couldn't keep hiding their meetings and so had told her family of him—news which had been met with very little excitement but no disapproval. Not only had Mr. Collin come the following week as promised, but he'd come once a week since. He was consistent, she'd give him that much. Not overly diverting, but certainly consistent.

Dinah closed her eyes. "I certainly wouldn't mind speaking with someone as handsome as Lord Lambert."

"Don't be vulgar," Eliza said.

"Why not?" Rachel asked. "It seems all of society expects it of us. Tell me you aren't blind to the way they watch us, waiting for us to slip up so they might laugh."

Eliza stood and crossed the room, coming to sit beside Rachel. "I'm not doing a very good job of shielding you both from it, I'm afraid."

"It isn't your responsibility to protect us from everything," Rachel said, resting her head down on an upturned fist. "I sometimes wish we'd never come to London."

"Good heavens." Dinah sat up, a lock of hair breaking free of its pins from the sudden movement and splaying over her shoulder. "We are *not* going to exchange a perfectly lovely conversation about a beautiful man like Lord Lambert with one regarding something as pitiful as what society thinks of us."

An unladylike guffaw pressed against Eliza's lips, begging to be let free. Instead, Eliza clamped her mouth shut and forced her brow down. She truly *ought* to remind Dinah not to speak so . . .

Only, Rachel's lips were pressed tightly to the side, and it looked like she was fighting the merriment, too.

"I say," Dinah intoned, "let society think what it will. I have far better things to worry about."

"Bravo," Lady Blackmore said, striding into the room. "Turning a slightly deaf ear toward society can only do one a world of good. Now girls, how was your at-home? I am sorry not to have made it."

"Well," Rachel pulled the word out. "Dinah and I made pleasant conversation with Lady Honeyfield and Lady Oakley, while *Eliza* . . ." Rachel let her voice trail off while Dinah waggled her eyebrows.

Oh, botheration. Eliza turned toward a perplexed-looking Lady Blackmore. "I spoke with Lady Augusta and Lord Lambert. That is all."

"Is it?" Lady Blackmore asked.

Not her, too.

"Certainly," Eliza protested.

"You three have certainly become thick as thieves," Lady Blackmore commented.

It was true. Eliza had been many times in the company of Augusta and Lord Lambert. Ever since the dinner party ten days hence, she'd seen her friends many times about Town.

"Perhaps," she said, trying to make it sound unimportant. "But, as I was just telling Rachel and Dinah"—she speared them both with her own look—"I only ever happen upon Lord Lambert when he is accompanying Augusta." Which, apparently, was all the time. She'd happened upon them at Almack's, at Lady Oakley's dinner party the day afterward, and they'd come to call on her at the same time this morning. She'd actually been quite unsure if they'd arrived together or not. Surely not, but it was a rather odd coincidence.

What she would never admit to her sister, cousin, or Lady Blackmore is that there had been many moments when she'd almost wished they weren't three, but two. Only she and Lord Lambert. Did that make her a terrible friend?

Eliza glanced up to see all three women watching her. "Truly, there is nothing for you all to smirk about." Not with Augusta always around, anyways. And why shouldn't she always be present? Augusta was of far higher birth than herself, she was far more beautiful, and certainly more charming.

"Then that is a shame," Lady Blackmore said, standing once

more. "But that gives you all the more reason to accompany us to Almack's tonight."

"Oh, no," Eliza said firmly. She hadn't been back since that first time when she'd accidentally tripped Lord Lambert—an incident she was happy to know had *not* been discovered by the gossipy hens of society. "I told you last week. I've gone once and have learned for myself it is not to my liking."

"You must come," Dinah said. "How would it look for Dinah and I to go, but not you, the eldest?"

"What happened to not caring about society?" Eliza asked.

Dinah actually had the gall to appear affronted. "What happened to looking out for us, your dearest family?"

Just at the thought of going back to Almack's, Eliza could feel the tightness in her stomach, the sickening heat creeping down the back of her neck. "There are plenty of other social events we might attend."

"But none other so full of beautiful men," Dinah said.

Eliza could not believe this. "You ridicule me when I give in, but you are angry at me when I don't."

Lady Blackmore walked over to her. "Please, dear, there is no need to be upset."

"I don't care to go," Eliza stated again. "I shall stay home with Father. You three are more than welcome to have a good time."

"It would be good for you to go, though," Lady Blackmore pushed.

The door flung open with a bang, and Father strode into the room. He didn't look at any of them but moved quickly toward the writing table near the window. "She doesn't have to go." He tugged a drawer open and rummaged through the contents.

"Can I help you find something, Father?" Eliza asked, relieved he'd chosen that moment to interrupt.

"I'm out of ink," he said.

With any luck, this could be just the thing to make everyone forget about Almack's. "I believe there's some in the middle drawer," she called to him.

He slammed the top drawer and yanked open the middle.

Eliza's brow dropped; at first, she'd just assumed he needed the ink to finish some matter of important business, but now he appeared more upset than anything.

"Good day to you," Lady Blackmore said, her tone hard and somewhat lofty.

"Good day." Father's tone was every bit as cold.

Eliza glanced over at Rachel and Dinah. The two were silent, but they eyed Lady Blackmore and Father with the same caution Eliza felt.

Rachel leaned in closer to Eliza. "Do you remember when you came home from riding Starfire yesterday afternoon and asked if anything had happened while you were away?"

Eliza nodded. She'd been told all had been quiet.

Rachel whispered, "We lied."

"I *believe*," said Lady Blackmore, "that your daughter would benefit from your encouragement just now."

"Encouragement to do what?" Father didn't look up from the drawer he was looking through, though he must have riffled through all its contents by now.

"To attend Almack's with us, of course."

He stood, an ink bottle in his hand. "If she doesn't care to go, then she doesn't have to."

"It wouldn't hurt for you to make an appearance, either."

"If I were ever forced onto the dance floor, I am quite certain it would."

Lady Blackmore picked up her skirt and stalked over toward him. "You said you wanted all three girls married by autumn. That will never happen if they and you are forever at home, avoiding society and new associations."

Though Father's tone stayed level, his face turned a shade of red Eliza had never seen on him before. "I have all the associations I care for, between home and White's."

"Exactly my point. You had no desire to attend White's at all when I first brought it up. I had to fairly drag you there. Now, you have found you quite enjoy the place."

"Nonsense—"

"If you say that word one more time to me"—Lady Blackmore's tone dropped to levels which could only purport danger—"I promise you, I'll have it etched in leather and baked inside an eel pie, and then I'll force you to eat it for dinner." Spinning about, skirts billowing around her, Lady Blackmore rushed from the room.

Father seethed. "A tongue enough for two sets of teeth, she has." He stomped over to the window, which faced the front drive, and peered through the lace curtains.

From where Eliza sat, she could hear the slam of a carriage door and then the rattle of wheels.

Muttering to himself, Father stormed out of the room.

"Good heavens," Eliza said. The tension in the air had not fully left with either Lady Blackmore or Father. If only she could open a window and air the room of tension as easily as she could a bad smell.

"It seems," Dinah said, "they have had a disagreement of some kind."

Eliza couldn't believe they'd not told her. "Apparently."

"Best we could piece together," said Rachel, "my uncle is finally fed up with being pushed to be something he's not."

"Aren't we all." Between Father's pride and Lady Blackmore's determination to see them all better off, Eliza wasn't surprised. Eliza could relate, but she couldn't help him know what to do about it. She was struggling with the same problem herself.

CHAPTER TEN

A dam leaned forward, resting his arms against his knees.

"Look!" Kitty said, stopping her spin only long enough to change directions. "Doesn't my new ribbon match my dress perfectly?"

"It most certainly does." At least, he thought so. But then, he wore whichever jacket he wished with whichever breeches, to the point that his aunt vocally washed her hands of him several times a month. So, who was he to say?

But so long as Kitty liked the ribbon he'd gotten her, he didn't care either way.

"Come along now, dear," Miss Notley said, placing a hand at Kitty's back.

"No." Her small face scrunched into a tight scowl. "I want to stay with Adam and meet his guests."

"You know such a thing is not proper." Miss Notley shook her head.

Kitty hurried over to Adam, flinging herself over his knee. "Please! I want to stay and meet the beautiful ladies and fine gentlemen."

Adam patted her back. "I haven't invited many, and you already know most of them."

"Who?"

"Come along, dear." Miss Notley's voice turned firm, even as she caught Adam's eye and gave him a subtle nod "no."

Though what could she possibly be telling him not to do? He understood that Kitty was far too young to be permitted to join him for dinner tonight. He wasn't about to give in, no matter how adorable she looked in her dress and purple ribbon.

"I've invited Lord and Lady Oakley and their two sons, Sir Mulgrave and his daughters and niece, and of course Lord and Lady Honeyfield, and Lady Augusta—"

"Augusta!" Kitty shot back up onto her feet like she'd been hit by lightning.

Miss Notley only glanced up at the ceiling, with a "now you've done it" sigh.

Kitty wrapped her arms tightly around Adam's leg. "I'm staying here until Augusta comes."

"Come now," Adam said, trying but failing to pull her off him. "It is time you head upstairs and ready yourself for bed."

"I don't care. I want to see my friend."

Adam looked over at Miss Notley, but the poor woman looked done in. He had heard rather a lot of noises coming from the nursery that day; no doubt, it had been a long one for Kitty's governess.

"Kitty," he tried again. "We have discussed this. It is important that you learn to obey."

"But Augusta is my friend."

"I know, and I'm sure she misses you. But tonight is for the grown-ups, dear. She can come see you another time."

"No!" Kitty held more tightly about his leg. If she held on any tighter, she was sure to cut off the circulation. "She never comes to see me anymore. She's always too busy seeing you."

Adam pulled back, allowing her to remain secured about his leg. As he understood it, while his father was alive, Lord Honeyfield had come frequently to visit, usually bringing Lady Augusta along to visit with Kitty. However, as of late, whenever Lord Honeyfield came for a visit, Lady Augusta stayed with the other adults or didn't come at all. He'd seen the way Kitty talked and talked whenever Augusta was around—did he really want to deny her such a sweet friendship?

"Very well," he said with a sigh. "I'll make you a deal."

Kitty's head came up, but she didn't lessen her hold.

"I'll allow you to stay and visit with the adults *if* you promise to be a very well-behaved girl and go straight up with Miss Notley the moment dinner is announced."

Kitty's head bobbed up and down as she quickly agreed. "I promise."

"All right then; stand up proper like. Lady Augusta will be here any minute now."

Not ten minutes later, not only had Lady Augusta arrived but so had nearly all of Adam's other guests. All, excepting the Mulgraves. Adam stood beside several of the gentlemen, or at least close enough to hear their conversation and join in occasionally, but also close enough to the front-facing window so that he might keep a look out for Miss Mulgrave. She had not been at Almack's several days previous, though Miss Dinah and Miss Chant both had been. He'd thought it a bit strange, so when he'd seen Sir Mulgrave at White's the next day, he'd asked after Miss Mulgrave. Her father had only said she'd wanted some time to herself. He sincerely hoped she wasn't ailing.

"Lord Lambert," Lady Augusta said, walking up to him, Kitty by her side. "I understand that this sweet girl has you to thank for the beautiful purple ribbon in her hair."

Kitty looked up at Lady Augusta, her smile bright. Clearly, allowing the girl to stay and see her friend again had been the right decision.

"It was a small matter," he said. He was happy to see Kitty so pleased, yet his gaze strayed again to the window.

"Are you expecting more guests?" Lady Augusta asked.

"Yes." Though he ought to be giving his attention to the ones who'd already arrived instead of staring out the window. "Sir Mulgrave, his daughters, and Miss Chant."

"Oh." Lady Augusta's eyes lit up. She bent down slightly as she addressed Kitty. "I cannot wait to introduce you to Miss Mulgrave. She is such a dear, and I just know you two will become fast friends."

The soft clatter of carriage wheels against pavement came from outside. Adam took a step closer to the window and looked out. A simple carriage pulled up to the front, the door opening before a footman could get to it. Though Adam looked down from above on those who stepped out onto the street, even from this vantage he knew it to be Sir Mulgrave. Miss Chant exited next, followed by Miss Dinah. Adam found himself holding his breath. Surely Miss Mulgrave wouldn't bow out of yet another social engagement, such as she had from Almack's.

Finally, Eliza stepped out. He didn't have to see her well to tell she looked lovely. Truth be told, she could have left her curls to go flat and worn a most drab dress, and Adam still would have thought her beautiful. Giving Lady Augusta and Kitty a quick "Excuse me," he made his way out of the room and toward the front door.

Halfway to the stairs, Adam paused.

What was he doing? He'd never before felt the need to be at the door when visitors or guests arrived. He had a butler—young though the man might be. He had footmen and maids to escort guests to the drawing room where they all gathered. Why rush to greet the Mulgraves?

But he wasn't rushing out to meet the Mulgraves, not all of them, anyway.

Miss Mulgrave was the only one he was truly thinking of.

Voices floated to him. Miss Dinah was speaking; he recognized her voice, though he couldn't make out the exact words. He glanced about him. He was standing, like a simpleton, in the middle of the corridor. That would never do.

Taking two long steps to his left, he moved up to the next flight of stairs which led to the floor above, the floor of guest bedchambers, and slipped into the shadows beneath. Hunched down low, he pressed himself up against the underside of the stairs just as the Mulgraves reached the landing.

"The guests are gathered in there," said Mr. Reid jovially.

"Thank you," Sir Mulgraves said, leading his daughters and Miss Chant the rest of the way toward the room.

Silently, Adam watched them enter. Miss Mulgrave still remained behind the others, her back toward him. She moved into the drawing room, and, lucky for him, stayed within easy viewing. Lady Augusta hurried over to her, and they gave one another a quick hug. Then, Lady Augusta introduced Miss Mulgrave to Kitty. The young girl's prim curtsy tugged at Adam's heart. He still was unsure how the girl had come to be in his father's care, but he could not deny that he fully understood how his father had come to be wrapped around the young girl's finger.

Watching Miss Mulgrave and Kitty speaking to one another, he could no longer deny something else as well. He was growing quite fond of Miss Mulgrave. More than fond, if he were being honest with himself.

Aunt Priscilla's warning came back to him. He was to find a woman equal to his status. One who could help the family. One who provided important connections and a sizeable dowry.

Miss Mulgrave had none of those things. Though he had told her not to worry, he wasn't blind to the fact that the Mulgraves were not well accepted by most. While society had been in awe at Sir Mulgrave's bravery in fighting off the highwaymen that had threatened Lady Blackmore, their admiration had not gone so far as to readily accept him into their ranks. If only society was a little less concerned about connections and titles, they'd see what he saw. A caring family. A kind and considerate woman.

Yet, here he was, hiding beneath the stairs—in his own house no less—spying on his guests.

What would happen if he chose to court Miss Mulgrave? Aunt Priscilla would not take kindly to it, of that he was certain. He'd had a handful of conversations with Sir Mulgrave at White's, but that didn't mean the man would approve of him paying his daughter much attention. Then there was Lord Honeyfield and Lady

Augusta. Though he didn't sense any partiality on the lady's side, he'd been growing more aware of Lord Honeyfield's subtle hints that their families should always "stay close."

When Adam had first realized what Lord Honeyfield was implying, it hadn't worried him. He, too, had been thinking he and Lady Augusta may very well suit one another. Had she not been the very angel he'd been hoping for? Someone to care for Kitty and elevate his family's connections?

But watching Miss Mulgrave smile while talking to Kitty, he couldn't help but feel something deep inside him yearning for her.

Suppose the angel he'd been given was not the angel he wanted?

CHAPTER ELEVEN

K itty was a delight. Eliza spoke with the young girl and Augusta until dinner was called. At that point, her governess, Miss Notley, came to collect her. Though Kitty clearly was upset at the idea of having to leave, she kept her smile up, followed obediently behind her governess, and left the room with enough poise to rival even Lady Blackmore.

Since Lord Lambert was master of the house, he was obliged to walk in with Lady Honeyfield. Eliza had rather been looking forward to seeing him tonight. She never seemed to tire of their conversations, nor of how they could speak on any topic, profound or mundane, and find enjoyment in it. Still, even as he escorted Lady Honeyfield to the dining room, he did seem to glance over at her and Augusta quite often.

Both Eliza and Augusta walked in with either of the Oakley sons. However, when Lord Lambert looked at first Augusta and then Eliza *yet again* during their soup course, Eliza started to wonder if there wasn't something more to his looks than a man simply happy to see his friends. He had a peculiar crease that hung across his nose, directly between his eyes. His glances were not casual and quick, rather, he seemed to first study one of them and then the other.

Though Eliza did her best to fight it, when he looked hard at Augusta, she couldn't quell all the heat it stirred in her. She'd never before in her life been prone to jealousy. Yet, she found herself, more and more, wishing for time alone with Lord Lambert. But that would have been selfish. Ridiculous. Nonsense, her father would call it. Because that's what it was.

But then, he looked at her.

As the servants removed the main dish and proceeded to bring out plates of fish, Eliza caught Lord Lambert's gaze on her, and it wasn't at all the kind of a look a man gives a woman who is only a friend. It wasn't at all the simple smile of familiarity. Was she simply imagining things, or was he beginning to feel the stirrings of something more?

Was she?

Eliza placed her fork down. She couldn't eat just now. Though the man to her right, Lord Down, spoke on about his time on the continent, traveling through Italy and Spain, Eliza barely heard more than every third word.

She'd never had to ask her heart before, but now it seemed she very well might be falling for a man. A *titled* man of elegant breeding and lofty expectations.

Was that nonsense as well?

She certainly wouldn't be asking Father. Though she loved him deeply, this was just the type of thing he'd use his favorite word to describe, and just the thought of someone—anyone—telling her these burgeoning feelings deep inside were ridiculous hurt. Still, the thought of acting on them terrified her yet more.

Finally, dinner was over, and the women stood to leave. Eliza didn't dare meet Lord Lambert's gaze. Things between them had shifted, for her at least, over the course of eating potato soup and lamb with roasted carrots. Until she had herself sorted out once more, she could only hope the drawing room had a comfortable chair pushed somewhere near a far wall where she could sit by herself and think.

Blessedly, there was one near a small table. Eliza made her way there, not bothering to explain herself to the other women. They all seemed rather wrapped up in their own conversations anyhow. Eliza was pleased that Dinah and Rachel were enjoying themselves, but her head was swimming too much to join in any conversations just at the moment.

Eliza dropped heavily into the chair, and the table shifted just slightly.

Odd. She hadn't thought she'd bumped into it, nor even so much as brushed against it with her skirts. Eliza peered at the piece of furniture, then down its legs. By the feet rested a small form, one in a lovely dress with purple ribbons in her blonde curls.

"Why, Miss Kitty," Eliza said, keeping her voice low enough that no one but the girl would hear her, "whatever are you doing in here?"

Miss Kitty sat up. "I wanted to draw with the ladies after dinner."

"You mean *withdraw* with the ladies after dinner?"

She nodded, her curls bouncing, though her ribbons did look a bit more limp than they had earlier that evening. One appeared to be almost undone completely.

"Miss Notley said I had to go to bed, but I didn't want to. So I hid down here."

The young girl wasn't even dressed for bed yet. Clearly, she'd slipped away before the governess had finished readying her.

Eliza took hold of Miss Kitty's arm and gently helped her stand. "We certainly enjoyed speaking with you before dinner tonight," she said, retying the loosest of the ribbons. "But a girl your age needs to be sleeping at this time of night. It is what is best for you."

"But I love Augusta. She's my friend."

Just then, Miss Notley peeked into the room. As soon as her eyes found Miss Kitty, she strode in, her mouth in a tight line.

"Come, Miss Kitty," she said. Though her voice was quiet, it was no less firm.

Miss Kitty wrapped herself around Eliza's arm most suddenly, both of her little arms encircling Eliza's.

"I want to stay," the girl said adamantly.

"No, Miss Kitty. It is time you returned to the nursery."

The dear held on to Eliza all the tighter. It was actually quite surprising the little girl could squeeze her arm so. If ever she set her mind to climbing trees, Eliza would not worry that the girl knew how to avoid falling.

"Miss Kitty?" Augusta said, turning atop the settee near the fire where she sat. "What are you doing down here, dear?"

"I wanted to draw . . . *withdraw* with the ladies."

Miss Notley addressed the room. "Please excuse us; I will see her up to bed immediately."

"Oh no," Augusta said. "Let her stay for a moment. She and I do not get enough time together as it is."

It seemed a rather bold statement for one who was not the lady of the house; nonetheless, no one disagreed.

Smiling at the girl, Augusta patted the empty seat beside her on the settee. Miss Kitty, instead of letting go of Eliza's arm, dragged her up and out of the chair, hauling her across the room and toward the settee as well. So much for a few quiet moments alone.

Even as Miss Kitty deposited Eliza on the settee, Augusta called back across the room, "You should join us as well, Miss Notley."

"Thank you, my lady," she said, curtsying and then taking the seat Eliza had only just vacated.

Miss Kitty crawled up onto the settee between Eliza and Augusta. She turned around, facing the other ladies, and sat up straight, her hands in her lap, her lips a perfect demure smile. It seemed Miss Notley, for all the handful Miss Kitty certainly was, still managed to instill quite a bit of etiquette into her small charge.

"We were just discussing how delicious tonight's potato soup was," Augusta said. "Were you able to enjoy some as well?"

"I was," Miss Kitty said, her tone most proper. "It was very delightful, was it not?"

Eliza smiled. "Most certainly it was."

"Almost as delightful as the company," Lady Honeyfield said. "It has been good to see you all again."

"Most certainly," Lady Oakley agreed. "We've even been able to see those we had not expected." She lifted an eyebrow and shot a glance over toward the far side of the room.

Eliza glanced over her shoulder to where Miss Notley sat, silent, her head bent down.

As the echo of voices and footfalls coming from the corridor reached them, foretelling of the gentlemen's slow progress toward the drawing room, Lady Oakley spoke on. "Miss Kitty, I do hope you learn as much as you can from the lovely Lady Augusta." Her nose turned up. "I cannot imagine you will have much to learn from your governess. Truly now," she shifted in her seat, as though addressing only Lady Honey-field while still speaking loud enough for the whole room to hear, "I find it very unwise to enlist the services of a woman who was unable to secure herself a husband to teach our daughters anything."

Eliza's jaw tightened. Though the insult had not been aimed at her, she still felt the sting. No one seemed to know what to say. Surely there was some witty comment Eliza could say, something that would take the attention away from Miss Notley, or even show support for her while not offending or causing more distress to anyone in the room.

"I do see what you mean," Lady Honeyfield said. Though she didn't openly object, her tone didn't sound like she agreed either.

At least someone was saying *something*.

But pacifying Lady Oakley was not enough. Someone needed to stand up for Miss Notley.

Eliza's mind jumped back to last spring, to standing there between the trees, watching her father take down all three highway-men. How could she call herself his daughter if she hadn't the courage to stand up to one woman?

"You'll have to forgive me," Eliza said, her words uncomfortably loud in her own ears, "but I *don't* see what you mean."

"I beg your pardon?" Lady Oakley seemed truly confused.

It wasn't going to be elegant, or witty, or droll, but Eliza knew she had to say something. "I don't see why you would make such an unkind statement. Miss Notley seems a very capable woman."

"One who cannot even manage to put her charge to bed," Lady Oakley muttered.

"Look at Miss Kitty. Clearly, she has been taught the proper way to sit, speak, and listen to others. The fact that she is friendly and kind shows she has been raised with a competent, kind hand. I think—"

The drawing room door opened, and the gentlemen walked in, causing Eliza to pause.

The sight of so many more people, albeit people Eliza knew at least a little, made her heart beat fast. She'd already been nervous to speak up; the growing audience only stole whatever bravado she may have mustered.

"I think," she said softly, "we ought to respect *all* people, no matter their current situation."

The gentlemen must have sensed there was more than easy gossip happening among the women, for they had quieted as well.

"Kitty," Lord Lambert said, moving up toward the settee. "What are you still doing up? I believe we had an agreement."

Augusta quickly stood. "You must not blame her. It was I who suggested she sit with us for a bit." She turned toward Miss Kitty. "But perhaps you ought to head back to the nursery now?"

Miss Kitty stood, as did Miss Notley. The governess hurried forward, even as Miss Kitty curtsied prettily for the group. Taking Miss Kitty by the hand, Miss Notley turned to walk her out of the room. She caught Eliza's eye just before slipping past her and mouthed a silent, "Thank you."

Eliza gave her a small nod. She wasn't at all sure her statement hadn't come out sounding far too self-righteous. But at least she'd said *something*. It hadn't been standing up to armed men, but she felt sure, had her father known the whole of it, he'd feel proud of her.

She was proud of herself.

CHAPTER TWELVE

Despite the room calming and easy conversation beginning moments after Miss Kitty and Miss Notley left, Eliza's heart continued to pound. She couldn't believe she'd actually stood up to someone—a titled woman no less—like she had. In the three-quarters of an hour that had passed since the exchange, Eliza had come up with no less than five things she'd wished she'd said differently.

She wished she'd sounded more refined, more polite.

She wished she could have said something witty . . . though she still hadn't been able to figure out what it could have been.

She wished she'd done a better job, was all.

Somehow, she didn't think Father thought back to that day on the road and wished he'd stopped the highwaymen differently. She needed to let the matter rest. It was done, and that was that.

As conversation grew, filling the room to bursting, Eliza was able to stand and slip back over toward the far side of the room. Hopefully, a bit of space would help her calm down and think clearly once more. She didn't sit as she had before, but instead moved closer to the window, reveling in the small draft which cooled her heated face.

"You were marvelous," Augusta said, striding toward her with Lord Lambert.

Together again. The two seemed nearly inseparable.

Eliza turned and faced them. She tried to smile but couldn't seem to get it to come out right.

"Thank you, I suppose," she said. "I'm afraid I rather made a mull of the whole thing."

"No, you didn't," Augusta insisted. "I'm so glad you stood up for Miss Notley. Someone certainly needed to."

Eliza only shrugged. But she was struggling to pull her gaze away from Augusta's arm, from the way it looped so comfortably through Lord Lambert's. They certainly appeared very much at ease with one another.

Her stomach sank; clearly, it was time she let go of any fledgling ideas that Lord Lambert might prefer her. Why should he? Yes, they enjoyed one another's company, but she could offer him nothing. Truth was, he'd be lowering himself in the eyes of much of society should he show her any true preference. Suddenly, Eliza felt quite tired, and not at all equal to staying.

"I only heard the very end of your performance," Lord Lambert said, "but I thank you as well. Lord Oakley is a good man, but his wife can be . . ."

"Judgmental," Augusta finished for him. "Though that's only because you don't know her well. Once you come to know her as well as I do, you realize the correct word is harsh."

"Why should she not be?" Eliza asked, her tone flat. "Does not the title that comes when marrying a baron also come with the right to look down on those less fortunate?" Where was Father? Eliza allowed her gaze to move about the room. She desperately wanted to return home.

"Eliza, are you all right?" Augusta asked.

"I'm sorry," Eliza said, stepping a bit to the side. "I think it is best we return home for the night." She took several steps toward Father, calling back over her shoulder. "Thank you for having us tonight, my lord."

Eliza hurried over to where Father was standing near the hearth, listening to Lord Honeyfield and Lord Oakley. She placed a hand against his arm and, when he bent her way, whispered quickly of her desire to leave. He gave her only a nod, but then quickly excused himself from the other gentlemen and motioned to both Dinah and Rachel. Not one of her family, it seemed, was overly surprised at her desire to leave early. Nor did they need to be asked to wait with her in the front entry for the carriage to be brought around.

Perhaps they were all feeling the disparity between themselves and those whom they now associated with.

The butler, a young man with a large smile, stepped up after several minutes of silence. "Your carriage is ready, sir." He bowed at Father first and then toward the women. "Ladies." He opened the door, and a cold wind rushed in.

Father hurried out the door, only this time, the footman was already standing in wait and had gotten the carriage door open before Father could even reach the bottom of the stairs. Though Eliza was last out of the house, and still several strides away, she thought she saw the traces of a triumphant smile on the footman's face. Father, for his part, even went so far as to tap a hand against the brim of his hat—a sort of salute to the quick-thinking manservant. Father's pride had never extended so far as to ignore when others deserved credit.

"Miss Mulgrave, a moment if you please."

Eliza turned to find Lord Lambert standing in the doorway, alone, and with no greatcoat or hat to fend off the cold.

At seeing her pause halfway down the steps, he hurried forward. "I hope you are not leaving upset."

Eliza struggled to find words; the warmth that his nearness brought seemed to push aside logical thought.

"Lady Oakley was a most unkind guest tonight," he continued. "But please do not hold it against me for having invited her."

"Of course not." Eliza bobbed a shallow curtsy. "Thank you again for the lovely evening." The words came out sounding every bit as rehearsed as they actually were. "If you'll excuse me, my family is waiting."

"A moment more." He reached out, taking hold of her arm.

"Yes?" Had she not, only earlier that night, been wishing for just such a moment with him? A conversation between only the two of them? Though she knew her family was waiting, she also couldn't find it in herself to wish the moment to end.

His smile turned slightly embarrassed. "I also wanted to applaud you one more time . . . for the things you said in there." He motioned back over his shoulder and toward the open door.

Eliza's face warmed considerably; unfortunately, while blushing did much to make one uncomfortable, it did nothing to protect one from the evening cold. Frightfully lamentable, that.

"You don't suppose I've landed myself in Lady Oakley's black books, do you?"

"Most likely. But even if you have, what of it?"

Eliza pressed her arms closer to herself; and to think, he stood out here beside her *without* a coat, and he still wasn't showing any signs of being cold. "Forgive me, my lord, but that may be true for you, as a viscount. But I am only the daughter of a knight. Lady Oakley's opinion will be widely known soon, and I will be left to feel the full brunt of her wrath. That, I'm afraid, is the cost of foolishly speaking one's mind."

"It wasn't foolish in the least."

The horse pulling their carriage stomped impatiently. Eliza twisted a bit to glance his way. "Oh? And what would you call it if not foolish?" At least her family was all inside the carriage with the door shut, no doubt to aid in keeping the heat in and the cold out. Lucky for Eliza, the door also kept them from giving her any impatient glances or contemptible stares.

"I'd call it noble," Lord Lambert said, moving a half step closer.

He stood near enough that she had to intently focus on not accidentally bumping into him. Warmth spread through her, and suddenly the night air didn't seem too cold in the least. How would it feel to lean ever so slightly to the side and brush against him? What would it be like to go so far as to purposely reach for him? His gaze held hers, his eyes glinting in the candlelight which spilled from the house.

"I'd call it bold," he said, leaning in so that his face neared hers.

What little air there was between them sparked, sending excited awareness coursing over her skin.

"Would you?" she asked. She had never been known for her wit and it seemed in such a situation as this she was even less capable than usual of coming up with something droll.

"I'd even go so far as to call it . . . audacious." His gaze flicked down to her lips.

Oh, heavens. "I don't think anyone has ever accused me of being audacious before."

"Haven't they?"

He was so close; the tension his proximity caused was something she'd never experienced. All Eliza could do was shake her head.

"Well, it appears your friends and family aren't close enough observers." Lord Lambert bent in yet closer and whispered in her ear, "For I have known you to be *quite* audacious at times."

He pulled away and seemed to pull all the air from her lungs at the same time. With a smile and a nod, he turned away and strode back into the house.

CHAPTER THIRTEEN

S itting beside Eliza on the settee, Dinah placed her hands on either side of her and leaned forward.

"You should have been there, Mr. Collin," she effused. "Our Eliza was magnificent."

Eliza, for her part, simply sipped her tea and stayed silent. It was Mr. Collin's regular day for a visit, and though they'd all expected him, Eliza silently wished he'd stayed away. She hadn't spoken up last night for the purpose of having the story bandied about her own home time and time again.

Dinah sat up straight. "I think we ought to respect *all* people, no matter their current situation," she quoted Eliza. "Isn't that just like her, though?"

What *was* just like her was the way Eliza's face burned at Dinah's praise.

Mr. Collin smiled, but it was polite and no more. "She *has* always been quite willing to look out for others. However," he shot Eliza a quick glance before returning his gaze to Dinah, "I do hope Lady Oakley doesn't cause trouble over it. I have spent more time with the titled and wealthy than you ladies, and I must confess, I am worried this will not end well."

Eliza agreed. Still, she couldn't bring herself to regret what she'd done. Miss Notley had needed a champion in that moment; though Eliza didn't feel she had done it well, she was glad she'd said something.

Lord Lambert, at least, had thought well of her for it. Oh, and the way he'd looked at her directly before she'd left? Eliza would never tire of the memory.

"What do you think, Eliza?" Rachel asked, forcing Eliza to focus once more on the conversation at hand.

If only her family would leave off talking about last night and change the topic to something less troublesome, Eliza could allow herself to think on that parting moment instead. It had been an intense moment, but one she hardly could make heads or tails of now. That she hadn't been granted a moment to herself all day wasn't helping either.

"I do not know Lady Oakley well enough to guess what she may say or do," Eliza said, "but I don't regret what I said last night."

Nor did she in any way regret her few moments alone with Lord Lambert. She didn't dare express her gratitude to Dinah and Rachel for closing the carriage door and granting her some privacy the night before—it would lead to embarrassing questions regarding why Eliza was so grateful—but she felt it all the same.

"Well," Mr. Collin leaned forward, placing his teacup back on the low table between them, "I for one am glad you left off when you did. As is, it was only a few sentences. Hopefully, Lady Oakley is feeling forgiving today and will let it rest."

Eliza suddenly felt two inches tall. "You aren't actually opposed to what I did?"

Mr. Collin shook his head from side to side. "More worried—worried this might not end well for you." The corner of his mouth ticked up, and he patted her arm. "Fear not, though. Wasn't Mr. St. John always saying that the angels make note of every good deed done and that the doers never go unblessed for long?"

Eliza smiled at the memory of the vicar who'd sermonized to them Sunday after Sunday.

"How is old Mr. St. John, by the by?" Mr. Collin asked, once more leaning back in his chair and addressing the room at large.

Eliza's gaze fell to the spot on her arm where he'd touched her. When they'd known each other in the past, his touch had most certainly elicited something inside her, but this time, she couldn't deny that she felt nothing at the contact.

"Oh, had you not heard?" Rachel spoke up. "He passed on. It was four years ago this May, I believe."

How was it that even though Lord Lambert hadn't reached for her the previous night, he still managed to set her heart racing and her skin tingling?

More importantly, had he felt the same?

Eliza sipped at her tea. There was a very real possibility the preference was on her side alone.

Dinah bumped Eliza's shoulder. Eliza blinked and looked about her. Mr. Collin, Rachel, and Dinah were all standing, and it seemed Mr. Collin was bidding them farewell.

Eliza quickly stood.

"It was a pleasure speaking with you ladies this morning," he said, bowing. "Until next week?"

"We look forward to it," Eliza said with a curtsy.

The moment the door closed behind Mr. Collin, leaving the three of them alone, Rachel turned toward Eliza. "Are you feeling unwell?" she asked. "You have not seemed yourself all morning."

"I am well," Eliza replied. She loved both her sister and her cousin dearly, but she wasn't about to tell them of feelings she'd only just admitted to herself. More still, she had very little faith such would ever be returned in kind.

"Worried Mr. Collin might be correct?" Rachel pressed.

"Perhaps a little." That was a good enough excuse, and right now she needed one. She also needed something to keep her from dwelling too long on last night's confusing, if thrilling, departure. For the longer she thought about the incident, the less confident she was that Lord Lambert had meant anything by it.

"Do you suppose," Eliza said by way of keeping their conversation off last night, "Lady Blackmore is still upset?"

"If she is," Dinah said, "she isn't the only one. Did you notice how quietly Father ate his breakfast this morning?"

Rachel dismissed the comment with a shrug. "He's always silent during breakfast."

Dinah shook a finger. "Yes, but it was the *way* he was silent."

"Then," Eliza said, "we ought to go visit Lady Blackmore, I think. She's far more likely to be upset than he, and if even Father is acting so morosely, then surely she will be even more so."

Not half an hour later, the three of them had donned pelisses and fur-lined bonnets—a frivolity they'd never enjoyed before Father had decided to spend his life's savings on this single London Season—and were at Lady Blackmore's door. The butler answered quickly and, knowing them quite well for all the times they'd visited these past couple of months, showed them directly into the parlor.

Lady Blackmore sat, gaze unseeing on the fire in the hearth, mouth set in a firm line, hands clasped tightly in her lap.

"Good day to you," Eliza said, hurrying over to the kind woman.

Eliza's words seemed to snap Lady Blackmore out of whatever reverie had held her attention. She smiled, and though it appeared sincere, Eliza didn't believe the lady was actually in good humor this morning.

"Hello, my dears," she said, greeting them each with a press of her cheek against theirs. "I am glad you've come to see me today. You know"—she motioned for them to sit and then took the chair beside the hearth once more—"I have heard rumors this morning of a very eventful night."

Oh, botheration. And here Eliza had hoped coming to see Lady Blackmore would be the perfect distraction from last night. Instead, she sat back, silent, as her words from last night were once again repeated by Dinah and Rachel. She was still glad she'd spoken up for Miss Notley's sake—she truly was—only her words sounded more and more self-righteous every time she was forced to rehear them. Awkward, too. If anyone in that room had been uncertain if she'd been raised to become a lady of the upper echelon before last night, they certainly knew she hadn't now.

"Eliza," Lady Blackmore said when the tale was finished. "I am ever so proud of you."

"Thank you, my lady."

"I thought I told you to leave off the 'Lady.' But never mind that now; I'm just sorry I was unable to join you all last night. I would have given anything to see you put Lady Oakley in her place."

"That was not my intention, I assure you," Eliza said. But her mind stayed on the fact that Lady Blackmore had not accompanied them last night. Eliza had not thought much about it at the time, but now that her mind mulled it over, it did strike her as rather odd that Lady Blackmore would not have been invited.

More likely, she *had* and had simply chosen not to go.

And the only reason Eliza could think that Lady Blackmore would have turned such an invitation down was to avoid a prideful man they all knew quite well.

"Pardon my boldness," Eliza said, her mind instantly jumping back to the previous night and the way Lord Lambert had called what she'd done *bold*. Echoes of heat caused her heart to race once more.

"Yes, dear?" Lady Blackmore prompted.

Eliza drew herself up. Here she was about to say something quite forward yet again. Perhaps Lord Lambert had been right—perhaps she could be more audacious than she'd known.

"I only wondered at not seeing you last night, nor today." Lady Blackmore very nearly always joined them for their at-home. "I wondered, or rather *we* wondered, if there wasn't perhaps some reason?"

Rachel lifted a single eyebrow, seemingly impressed with Eliza's straightforwardness. Or perhaps she was just surprised. Dinah, for her part, kept her gaze on Lady Blackmore, clearly eager to hear her reply.

"I hope you don't mind terribly," Lady Blackmore said with a smile and a shrug. "I had a small headache last night and slept late this morning."

In for a penny, in for a pound, as they said. "Did your headache have anything to do with your last conversation with our father?" Eliza pressed.

Now, Rachel was giving her two raised eyebrows and a look which clearly said she was *both* impressed and surprised.

Lady Blackmore lifted her gaze to the ceiling and shook her head. "I suppose there's no reason to deny it. Not to you three, leastwise."

"Why don't you come back home with us?" Rachel said. "If you and my uncle talk, surely you can patch things up and go back to the way they used to be."

Lady Blackmore placed an arm around Rachel, pulling her closer in. "I'm afraid not. I've thought it all out in my mind. I know what I *want* to say, and I know how he'll respond, and no matter how I've turned it about in my head, I can't see a pleasant ending to such a conversation."

"I doubt it is as bad as all that," Dinah said.

"You are young still," Lady Blackmore said. "You have yet to learn just how permanent poorly spoken words can be."

"Perhaps I am too young," Dinah said, a small huff to her words, "but I know Father is miserable, too. Surely that should give you some hope."

It gave Eliza hope. Lady Blackmore and Father had always had something of an unusual friendship. She was so proper and well-bred. He had worked all his life. She was charming and polite. He was often silent and when not, direct almost to a fault.

"You know I didn't mean it that way," Lady Blackmore said. "You are all like daughters to me now. I only meant that . . . in my *many* years, I have now and then said things I later regretted. I'm afraid I've already done so twice with your father, and I'd hate to make it a third."

Eliza could not like the idea of them staying as they were now. She loved her father, and she loved Lady Blackmore; she couldn't imagine them staying enemies. "Perhaps if you just tried?"

Lady Blackmore looked at each of them one by one, then sighed. "It's like this. I would start by saying it was good to see him again. Then, he'd probably grunt or simply nod my direction, which would only gall me. That would cause me to say something like, 'Am I impeding your ability to raise your daughters as you see fit simply by greeting you?' He, of course, would finally respond, but it would only be to say, 'That depends on why you're here.'" She let out a small huff.

It seemed Lady Blackmore had, indeed, worked it all out. "What would happen then?" It felt slightly wicked asking as much, but hearing Lady Blackmore voice the whole imagined conversation aloud was too diverting.

"I would say, 'If I have come to spirit your daughters away to either a shop or a social gathering, then surely you can have nothing but gratitude, as this is exactly what you, yourself, said you most hoped for.' Then he'd say, 'I want them married and settled, not shopped around like yesterday's fish.'"

A snicker escaped Dinah. Eliza had to roll her lips inward to keep from smiling too broadly. None of them should be finding this much enjoyment in a friend's distress.

"'They're not fish,' I would tell him, 'and I don't treat them as such.' But of course he'd come back with, 'But society does. If you'd just leave us be, we'd get along just fine, thank you very much.' And I'd say, 'At least you're expressing some gratitude now.' And then what do you suppose he'd say next?"

She paused, looking affronted with pursed lips and a raised brow. "He'd say, 'Nonsense,' and I would have nothing left but to storm from the room once again." Lady Blackmore let out an angered groan. "I never before thought I could loathe a single word so entirely."

Dinah laughed aloud this time. Even Rachel giggled softly.

"He does say it quite frequently," Eliza agreed.

"And it makes me more upset every time I hear it," Lady Blackmore said, shaking her head. "So you see, dears, it really is pointless."

"But suppose he doesn't respond in all those ways?" Eliza pressed. "Suppose he's upset about you coming to loggerheads too?"

Lady Blackmore only sighed again. "I have thought out a dozen more conversations, all slightly different, but all leading to the same end."

"With Father saying nonsense," Dinah said, finally getting control of herself once more.

"Precisely." Lady Blackmore's eyes flashed as she spoke.

"Could you perhaps find it within yourself to *not* leave the room, even if he says that word?"

"Doubtful. I'm afraid he's not the only one with a bit of pride. I think the best course of action is for me to stay away for a bit."

"Oh, no," Rachel said, sitting up and pulling away enough to face Lady Blackmore fully. "What will we do without you?"

Lady Blackmore turned toward Eliza with a mischievous smile. "Tell off pompous neighbors, it appears."

CHAPTER FOURTEEN

A dam swirled the brandy in his cup. The liquid reminded him of Miss Mulgrave's eyes. Though truth be told, he didn't need the reminder. He'd had a hard time thinking of anything else all day.

Sitting in White's, across from the enchanting lady's father, also didn't help.

"I must say again how pleased I was you and your family could join us last night," Adam said.

Sir Mulgrave only nodded.

Adam eyed the man. Though he was graying along the edges and his age was making its presence known in a few small wrinkles about his eyes, he was in no way old. He still held himself better than many far younger men Adam knew. Perhaps it was the result of working all his days. Or perhaps it came from having set his mind to lifting his family out of poverty. Either way, Sir Mulgrave bore himself well.

That being said, he wasn't doing an overly fine job of hiding the fact that something was bothering him. Was it the things Miss Mulgrave had said to Lady Oakley? Adam believed he knew Sir

Mulgrave well enough to know he wouldn't insist his daughter keep her kind opinions to herself. Quite the opposite, in fact.

Still, *something* was wrong. "Did you enjoy yourself last night, sir?" Perhaps if he started there, he would figure out what was wrong.

"Yes."

Lud, not even a 'thank you, my lord' at the end. Sir Mulgrave wasn't usually one to add unnecessary syllables to his statements, but Adam had expected more than a one-word answer.

He needed to be more direct. "Was your daughter upset by the things Lady Oakley said?"

Sir Mulgrave looked up from his drink, confusion evident in his expression.

"When Lady Oakley said some unkind things of Miss Notley."

Sir Mulgrave blinked but still said nothing.

"And your daughter spoke up on her behalf."

"Oh, that." Sir Mulgrave shook his head. "Between you and me, I wasn't the least bit surprised. Eliza is generally reserved and keeps her opinions to herself, but she's never been able to *not* help someone in need."

It put Adam firmly in mind of a man he knew who had saved a lady—one he'd never before met—from three highwaymen, no matter that it put his own life in jeopardy.

But Adam simply settled for saying, "I admire that about her."

Sir Mulgrave only grunted and took a small drink from his glass, once more returning to the vacant staring he'd been engaged in only moments ago.

At least the man wasn't upset with his daughter.

Eliza.

It was a beautiful name, and it fit her well, too. Simple, straightforward, yet elegant in its simplicity.

"You aren't put out that she chose to do so in your house, are you?" Sir Mulgrave asked suddenly, his head swinging back around; he eyed Adam with a disapproving glower.

"Gads, no," he said quickly. He truly and honestly thought more of Eliza for what she'd said, not less.

"Eliza may be gentle," Sir Mulgrave continued, "but she's strong when she needs to be."

"I've seen that myself."

"Oh?" Sir Mulgrave slowly lowered his drink onto the table, his gaze never leaving Adam. "And just *when* have you seen as much?"

Whatever had been bothering the man before, it appeared forgotten. Adam clearly had all of Sir Mulgrave's attention now.

"As I said," Adam sputtered, "last night, with Lady Oakley."

"Any other time?"

Adam had never realized how intimidating one could be when simply sitting and staring. No matter that he and Sir Mulgrave had a well-established acquaintance, Adam wasn't about to discuss the way Eliza made him feel, not with his own family or friends and certainly not with Eliza's own father. Not when Adam himself was still sorting out what to do about it all.

"We've shared many conversations," Adam answered truthfully, but without divulging more than was safe. "She's always spoken well of others, and she's told me enough about her childhood for me to know how willing she is to sacrifice for her family."

Sir Mulgrave watched him for a bit, then slowly rested back in his chair.

The sooner Adam moved their conversation away from Eliza, the better. "I only wondered if *you* were upset with her. You are clearly ill-at-ease over something."

"Another lady entirely," Sir Mulgrave muttered.

A lady, was it? That sounded intriguing—and like a much safer topic. "One that has earned your gall?"

"It is of no matter." Sir Mulgrave coughed, noisily shifting about in his chair. "You were saying you and Eliza often speak with one another?" He seemed as eager to change the subject as Adam had been moments ago.

"Now and again." Adam wasn't about to back down. "But this lady you are put out with. Is she someone I know?"

Sir Mulgrave shook his head. "I suppose. But she is nothing to you, I gather. Tell me of your conversations with Eliza."

Oh no, Adam wasn't going back to that. "What are conversations made of? This and that—the weather and fashions and on-dits. How can you be sure this lady you are put out with is nothing to me? My aunt has many connections."

"Not that high. What on-dits has Eliza shared with you?"

"Nothing of any note. And my aunt's connections run wide and far."

"Regardless of her connections, what . . . weather has caught my daughter's attention?"

He wished to avoid discussing his mysterious lady so much that he was bringing up what his daughter thought of the weather? Adam only stared at the man, one eyebrow raised.

Sir Mulgrave met Adam's gaze, holding it as though daring him to continue their pointless back and forth. Finally, Sir Mulgrave huffed. "You clearly have nothing more to say about Eliza, it seems. And I have nothing more to say about . . . the other lady. Let us leave it at that."

Very well then. They both fell silent, the din around them filling the space but not alleviating the bit of awkwardness that had also settled there. Adam never had considered Sir Mulgrave prone to beat about the bush, but neither had he ever been on the receiving end of the man's bluntness.

Would his own father have been like that?

He glanced over his cup at the man sitting across the table. Is this what it would have been like to sit with his own father, discussing Town and their acquaintances with one another? His father, who had all but ignored his own son, but had doted on a little girl? The hurt from that realization had begun to fade these past few weeks, at least. He understood why the man would have sent him to live with Aunt Priscilla. Many a man, finding himself a widower, would ask his late wife's family to care for his children. It was a frequent, even customary, occurrence. Adam was far from being the exception in that regard.

Moreover, though he didn't know the particulars that had led to it, Adam could understand why his father had come to care so much for Kitty. That dear, mischievous girl seemed to wend her way into *everyone's* heart. Even Aunt Priscilla was beginning to soften toward the girl.

Which reminded him, there was one other thing Adam *did* wish to speak to Sir Mulgrave about. "Might I ask you a question of an entirely different nature?"

Sir Mulgrave only glanced his way.

"It is in regard to Miss Chant."

"Rachel? What could you possibly need to ask in regard to her?"

It didn't slip past Adam that Sir Mulgrave had almost seemed to expect that Adam had something specific to say about Eliza yet was wholly surprised that he'd bring up Miss Chant.

"It is my understanding," Adam began, "that she is your sister's daughter?" Eliza had told him as much. By the way she had spoken of it, the topic did not seem like an overly sensitive one. Hopefully, Sir Mulgrave was of the same mind.

"Yes, when my sister's husband passed on, I offered to have her daughter come live with us. I knew finances would be tight for my sister, and Rachel had always been close to my own two daughters."

Adam nodded; he'd known as much already. At one point, one of the rare moments when it had only been the two of them, Eliza had gone further and admitted that her uncle had died in Marshalsea. Adam wasn't the least bit surprised that Sir Mulgrave was reluctant to admit as much.

"Did Miss Chant, when she first arrived, resent you? Perhaps for supposedly taking the place of her own father or for removing her from her home?"

Understanding dawned in Sir Mulgrave's eyes. "You are concerned for Miss Kitty."

Adam nodded. "When I first arrived, she hated me. Then we talked a bit, I bought her some ribbons, and for the past week or two, we have gotten along quite well. Then, this morning, she was suddenly back to hating me. I can't seem to figure her out."

"Nearly two weeks in her good graces, you say? My boy, sounds like you should be advising me. When Rachel first came to us, she was blue-deviled for months. Eventually, she started to look happier.

But even then, she was often sad or despondent." His voice grew soft as he picked up his drink. "I think Eliza did more to help her adjust than any of us."

Perhaps he ought to be having this conversation with her, then. Just the thought of seeing Eliza again made him feel strangely light-headed, as though he'd downed the contents of his drink in a single gulp.

"Make sure she knows you love her."

"Pardon me?" Adam's head snapped up. Had he heard Sir Mulgrave correctly?

"You said bringing her ribbons worked before." Sir Mulgrave gave him a one-handed shrug. "Maybe something like that would work again."

Miss Kitty. *Of course.* Adam lifted his glass to his mouth, more as a means of disguising his expression than anything. For a fraction of a moment, he'd thought Sir Mulgrave had been talking of Eliza. *Make sure she knows you love her.* Blast, was Adam really that far gone already?

By the time he'd taken a sip and set his glass back down, he was fairly sure he knew the answer.

Yes, he was.

"Thank you, sir," Adam said, standing. "I think that is exactly what I shall do." He smiled as Sir Mulgrave stood to bid him farewell. Sir Mulgrave was no doubt unaware of the double meaning in Adam's words. Still, the more Adam thought it over, the more he believed it the best course of action. He wasn't ready to declare himself—not yet. But letting Eliza know in more subtle ways seemed a wise move. With any luck, his attentions would not go unnoticed. More still, her reaction would let him know if estab-lishing something more permanent would be well-received.

With his head swimming as though he'd drunk several glasses of brandy instead of simply sipping at one as he had, Adam hurried home to begin his planning in earnest.

❦

Eliza tugged on the sleeves of her riding habit, then smoothed it over her stomach. Lord Lambert's invitation to go riding with him this morning had been a bit of a surprise, but one she was eager to accept.

"Do you suppose we will be warm enough?" Rachel asked, fiddling with her own riding habit as they all stood in the drawing room, waiting for Lord Lambert to arrive.

"You and I might feel the morning nip," Dinah said, "But I doubt Eliza will."

"What do you mean by that?" Eliza asked, looking up from her riding habit. She was just in time to catch the tail end of a shared look between her sister and cousin.

Eliza felt her face warm . . . *again*. She'd never in her life blushed half so often as she had since coming to London. Perhaps when this debacle was finally over, given a few months, of course, her face would finally return to her natural non-red complexion.

Dinah moved toward the window and looked out for the dozenth time. "I think that's him coming now."

Eliza's stomach flipped. "Are you sure?" Botheration—that had sounded far too eager. Even she heard it.

Dinah and Rachel shared another look.

Eliza chose to ignore it. Anything she said would only fuel the fire.

"It's either him," Dinah said, not bothering to hide the laughter in her tone, "or other men of the *ton* have taken to wearing the worst of all ensembles."

It was him. Eliza ducked her head and tried to appear as though she was fiddling with her habit once more; in truth, she was simply smiling too big for her own safety.

The butler announced Lord Lambert, and soon they were all mounted and headed toward Hyde Park. The morning air was crisp and there were even some chirping birds to be heard.

"Don't you think Eliza looks lovely today?" Dinah asked Lord Lambert as they turned a corner and the park came into view.

Eliza's stomach dropped. Had her sister truly just said that? Had she no decorum?

"Yes," Lord Lambert said, "She looks quite well today, as do you all."

The worst part of having a sister dig for a compliment was that now Eliza could not trust the things Lord Lambert said. Of course he had to compliment her after what Dinah had asked. It didn't mean he actually thought she looked nice.

Dinah, tugging her own horse up closer to Lord Lambert, only smiled more broadly. "Thank you, my lord, but Eliza far outshines us all."

Eliza, who was on Lord Lambert's other side, leaned over her horse, hoping to catch Dinah's eye and scowl her into silence.

No such luck.

"She has the sweetest temperament," Dinah continued, "and rides most elegantly. Do you not agree?"

Even as Lord Lambert turned at Dinah's bidding to see just how 'elegantly' Eliza may or may not ride, Eliza looked away. She turned her head far enough to the other side that hopefully, Lord Lambert would not catch sight of her mortification.

"You do not tell me anything I don't already know," Lord Lambert said.

It was a polite answer, but Eliza couldn't help but wonder . . . was there more than a little sincerity in there as well?

She faced forward once more but glanced around the brim of her hat at him. Had he meant it in earnest?

Their horses trod through the opening of the park and they were instantly surrounded by green.

Rachel, bless her, called to Dinah. "Do you see those purple flowers over there? Wouldn't it be fun to gather a few for our hair for dinner tonight?"

Dinah seemed hesitant to leave but finally acquiesced. As her sister and cousin made to leave, Eliza mouthed a silent 'Thank you' to Rachel, who smiled briefly before turning her horse and leaving them. When Eliza had envisioned what having a Season might mean, she'd never dreamed how embarrassing her sister and cousin could make it.

Alone, Eliza and Lord Lambert rode on at a slower pace. First, they talked of the beautiful morning. Then the conversation flowed naturally to their mutual love of horses. As they came to a stop beneath a large tree, they spoke of family.

"You'd had no notion before arriving at the London house?" Eliza asked. She'd known of Miss Kitty for some time now but hadn't heard the whole story.

"Not an inkling," Lord Lambert said, dismounting and looping his reins around a branch. "I was nearly speechless with surprise."

"Little wonder."

Lord Lambert walked over to her and placed his hands on either side of her waist. His gentle touch sent heat coursing over her. Eliza placed her hands atop his shoulders as he easily lifted her down from Starfire.

He didn't pull away when her boots reached the grass. Neither did she.

"Sometimes, I haven't the first idea what to think about Kitty. She's a dear girl, and I have no desire to send her away. Yet . . ." His head rocked from side to side. "I also don't know where she came from." Had he just pulled Eliza a fraction closer? "Between you and me, I think I'm afraid to admit to my staff that I don't know Kitty's true connection with my father, to admit that I—his heir—am not sure if she's my half-sister or something else entirely."

"If your father chose not to tell you, then how can they fault you for not knowing?"

"Logically, you are correct. But as master of the house, it seems like something I *ought* to know already." He chuckled at himself. "Ridiculous, I know."

Stepping back, he took her hand and slipped it around his arm.

Standing so near him, feeling his hands on her waist, and now walking side by side, it all felt natural. Comfortable.

As they neared Black Beard, he stretched his nose out toward Eliza. She stroked it softly.

"I don't know that I've ever met a more gentle horse," she said.

"Yes, some terror of the sea he turned out to be," Lord Lambert said, shaking his head. "Come on, Black Beard, old man. Show her how tough you can be, or she'll think we're both ninnies."

Black Beard huffed at Lord Lambert and then turned back to Eliza, nuzzling his nose against her hand.

Eliza laughed. "So much for that."

Lord Lambert cast a gaze upward. "And here I was depending on him to impress you." But she could tell he was smiling.

"Then he has done exactly that," she said. "A horse only shows love when he's been given much love first." She brought her face closer to Black Beard's. "Isn't that right?"

Eliza stroked Black Beard's neck. Though she was not willing to admit to more than that just now, the truth was, she adored horses and would never think highly of anyone who saw them only as work animals meant to be used but never loved.

"So you know," Eliza said, finding it easier to speak her heart when looking at Black Beard instead of straight at Lord Lambert, "I don't think it's ridiculous."

Lord Lambert didn't respond.

Eliza took in a breath and faced him. "You're still reeling from the shock of having a ward. You're still needing to establish yourself as master over a staff you've never met in a house you told me you couldn't even remember."

"My father would have sorted things out by now."

"Would he have? How can you be so certain? You hardly knew the man, so I believe it would be ill-advised to start assigning him so many enviable attributes that he becomes more hero than mortal."

Lord Lambert gave her a half-smile. "Perhaps you are right."

She squeezed his arm beneath her hand. "You will need to ask about Kitty eventually. Such knowledge cannot be avoided forever."

"On that, I *know* you are right." He placed a hand atop hers. "Do you ever wish you could go back to your life before everything changed?"

Eliza nodded. They'd both faced some life-altering upheavals the past few months. "Sometimes. Other times, I realize how blessed I am. After all"—she smiled, hoping he would too—"if not for the changes in both our lives, we wouldn't be enjoying this lovely morning together."

"That does make all the upheaval more worthwhile, doesn't it?"

They walked across the grass, still speaking of all the changes and uncertainties that made up their lives. But standing together, Eliza felt that things were, at least for the moment, a bit more right.

CHAPTER FIFTEEN

This time, when Lady Blackmore invited them all to attend a ball hosted by a friend of hers, Eliza didn't even hesitate before saying yes. Lady Blackmore and Father were still not speaking to one another, but at least the generous woman was willing to come visit again. She'd even joined them for their at-home earlier that week. Though Father had chosen to not attend this evening, he'd not so much as raised an eyebrow when Rachel, Dinah, and Eliza had asked for permission to join Lady Blackmore.

Just the same, the moment Eliza stepped into the ballroom, more crowded than any ball she'd yet attended, she knew it wasn't only for Father and Lady Blackmore that she'd agreed to come.

She was hoping to see Lord Lambert.

Their last conversation had left her confused—but it was a wondrous, thrilling kind of confusion. She'd never thought such a thing possible, yet here she was, quickly looking over every face in the gathered assembly, hoping to see one and one alone.

"There you are," Augusta said, walking over to her quickly, Lady Honeyfield with her.

"Good evening to you both," Eliza said, as her family also shared their greetings.

"Dinah, you look positively radiant this evening," Augusta said.

Dinah beamed. "Thank you, but I cannot take much credit. Lady Blackmore helped me to choose this fine gown, and Eliza did my hair. So you see, you truly ought to be praising them."

"Your own sister did your hair?" Lady Honeyfield asked, her tone falling a bit flat.

Eliza felt her face heat, but she kept her chin up.

Lady Blackmore, however, was quicker to speak. "Yes, she did, and does she not clearly have a fine hand?"

"Indeed." Lady Honeyfield didn't sound any more pleased. Her gaze caught on someone just to Eliza's right, and she bid them farewell, clearly eager to part ways.

Eliza was not sad to see the woman leave. They'd come to something of an understanding—albeit an unspoken one. Eliza did her best to remain as poised and polished as she possibly could in the woman's presence, and for her part, Lady Honeyfield didn't spend too much effort reminding Eliza she didn't actually fit into society.

Augusta looped her arm through Eliza's. "Would you come get some punch with me?" She leaned in and whispered, "I have something to say to you."

"May I?" Eliza asked Lady Blackmore; she was their chaperone for the evening, after all.

Lady Blackmore gave her permission, and Eliza and Augusta hurried off.

"Well?" Eliza pressed.

Augusta glanced about her first. "Your outburst the other night has quite inspired me. I have not been able to think on anything else."

This again? "It was not all that."

"I assure you it was."

Was speaking her mind truly so much of a surprise that *everyone* present had thought it noteworthy? *Oh, dear.* Perhaps Eliza had stepped further out of line than she'd realized. She looked about her. Several matrons were watching her movement across the ballroom.

Anytime Eliza went out in public, eyes followed her about, but she felt certain there were more tonight.

Her gaze caught hold of Lady Oakley, who watched her with a critical eye. The woman's lips pursed in a displeased pout before she turned to her neighbor and began talking quickly, motioning toward Eliza as she did so.

Perhaps Eliza *should* have stayed home with Father.

Of course, then she would have missed Lord Lambert. She was so eager to see him that even braving the critical judgment of the *ton* was a cost she was willing to pay.

They reached the punch table, and each ladled some punch into a cup.

"Do you remember when we first met?" Augusta asked.

"Certainly." Eliza tried to focus on her friend and not on the many stares aimed her way. Or, on the fact that she'd yet to see the one man she so desperately wanted to. Would he even be here tonight? She thought he came most weeks, but she herself had not come often enough to know that for sure.

"I told you I wanted to go riding through Hyde Park at the fashionable hour."

Eliza nodded.

"Well, I have very nearly decided to ask Lord Lambert if he might take me."

Eliza's eyes widened. "Ask him yourself?" Even she knew how impertinent such a thing would be.

"Yes," Augusta said, emphatically. "It is as you said. Sometimes a woman must stand up and ask for what she wants."

Had Eliza said that? She remembered something along those lines, but with so many women—and now men, too—watching her, Eliza felt more like crawling into a hole than encouraging her friend to face such censure as she was.

Of course, Lord Lambert chose that moment to appear.

"Good evening." His smile was every bit as handsome as she remembered. And the way his gaze held hers felt very nearly scandalous. He turned slightly to the side, where his aunt, Mrs. Bartlett, stood. "Aunt Priscilla, you know Lady Augusta, and you remember Miss Mulgrave from the other night."

"Oh, I remember," she said, sotto voce.

Eliza curtsied even as Augusta and Mrs. Bartlett did the same. It seemed Lord Lambert's aunt was part of the quickly growing group of matrons who did not approve of a young lady speaking contrary to an elder.

"The weather has turned a bit warmer as of late, has it not?" Augusta said.

"Yes, it has been quite pleasant," Lord Lambert said. Eliza could feel his gaze on her, though she kept hers averted.

"I was thinking only this morning," Augusta continued, "that it has been ages since I've been out for a ride in a carriage. Now that it's warm once more, I do miss it."

At least Augusta hadn't come right out and demanded Lord Lambert take her riding. Eliza should not have worried. While she herself couldn't seem to make her opinion known without eliciting the disapproval of an entire assembly—so many people were still staring at her—Augusta had enough poise to know better. She, at least, could express herself demurely. She could say what she wished without garnering the censure of the *ton*.

Eliza kept mostly to herself as Augusta and Lord Lambert carried the bulk of the conversation. Even Mrs. Bartlett seemed content to let the two of them do most of the speaking. But similar to Lady Honeyfield, she didn't forgo every opportunity to scowl at Eliza and subtly let her know how very unwelcome she'd become. Weeks of trying her best to fit in, and after only one little misstep, Eliza had been summarily rejected. At least, that's how it felt.

"Will you join us?" Augusta asked at length, after deftly getting Lord Lambert to agree to take her out in two days' time, and without once stepping outside the bounds of propriety. It was a wonder—one that left Eliza feeling completely inadequate.

"Perhaps," was all she could manage to say. She did love riding; though this would be in a carriage and not on horseback, the idea still held appeal. But, just now, she was wishing herself far away from the crowded ballroom and was too distracted to make plans for a future date.

"Well, let me know either way," Augusta said with a smile.

At least Eliza still had one friend.

Lord Lambert watched her carefully. "Would you care to dance, Miss Mulgrave?" he asked, stretching his arm toward her. "The musicians are only just starting the next set. If we hurry, I believe we can join in time."

Eliza's heart leapt into her throat. She'd danced but rarely the few times she'd been in attendance at Almack's, and never had she attended a ball other than there. Though Lady Blackmore had gone so far as to hire a dancing instructor for them, Eliza was fully aware of her own inadequacy.

Subtly, she shook her head. Country assemblies were one thing, but a grand ball such as this was quite another. "Are you not still in mourning, my lord?" she hedged.

"Perhaps, but I am nearing the end." His arm was still outstretched. "No one will think ill of it."

A gentlemen could always get away with more than a lady; if Eliza had been in mourning, she would have had to cast off her dark ensemble for certain before she entertained the thought of dancing.

Still, she could not like the idea. Not because he was still in mourning, but because she'd only be placing herself in easier view of the gathered assembly.

"I thank you," Eliza said, "but I cannot leave Augusta." If this many people were watching her, scrutinizing her now, the number would surely double if they had to endure watching her stumble through a dance.

"My aunt will keep her company. Is that not right?" Lord Lambert said, glancing Mrs. Bartlett's direction.

"Do not press the girl," his aunt replied. "She is correct in thinking that you shouldn't, as you *are* still in mourning. You don't wish to make the girl unhappy."

Apparently, the one who would be most unhappy if they danced was Mrs. Bartlett.

"Well, I agree with Lord Lambert," Augusta said. "A gentleman is expected to see to the future of his title and so, naturally, he cannot stand idly by at *every* gathering."

Eliza felt her face grow hot at Augusta's insinuation. "Is it not also expected that one not desert her friend?" Eliza ground out.

Augusta only sighed. "Go on." She gave Eliza a push, nearly sending her crashing into Lord Lambert. "I shall be quite happy here."

If she hadn't been blushing before, Eliza certainly was now. Still, her friend was giving her no way out. Eliza took Lord Lambert's offered arm, and they began walking across the floor toward where other dance partners were lining up.

"Are you truly that opposed to dancing with me?" Lord Lambert asked, his lips close to her ear.

A thrill shot down Eliza's back. Though pleasant on its own, the feeling mixed with the unease of so many eyes on her made her stomach churn.

"It is not *you* I object to."

"Then what?"

"It is the dance itself," she said, keeping her voice soft enough only he would hear. "Have you not noticed how they all stare?" Her steps slowed and he did the same, even taking a brief moment to glance about.

"It is not uncommon for a lovely woman to be much looked at."

Eliza stopped fully, facing him, her lips in a tight line. "Truly? You're going to start lying to me now?"

"When I said you were lovely I *wasn't* lying."

"Thank you, but you know that's not why they're staring."

He let out a sigh, even as the dance began in earnest behind him. "Perhaps a turn about the balcony instead? It is as Lady Augusta said before, and the night is not terribly cold."

"A chance to get away from the constant onlookers?" Eliza asked. "It could be well below freezing, and I'd still agree to go."

He looped her arm around his once more, and they changed direction, heading instead toward the open doors which led to the grand balcony.

They made it no more than two paces, however, before being stopped by Lord Down.

"Miss Mulgrave," he said jovially, a woman Eliza had never before met on his arm. "I am rather surprised to see you this evening."

"Is that so?" Eliza asked, fully aware she didn't know the other woman's name. But how did one go about reminding a gentleman to introduce her? Would asking outright be as ill-thought-of as her statement to Lady Oakley? She wasn't so good as Augusta to know how to subtly ask for what she wanted.

"I did not know your family was acquainted with our host," Lord Down continued. "After all . . ." He left off with a shrug. Bidding them no more farewell than that, he angled himself and the lady away and strode off. As he left, he did not lower his voice, and Eliza—and no doubt Lord Lambert—heard his words clearly. "I heard she actually did her own sister's hair before coming tonight. Can you imagine?"

"How very odd," the lady said, shooting Eliza a glance over her shoulder. "Not at all the type of person one expects to be invited to such an esteemed ball as this."

"Not at all," Lord Down agreed.

Eliza's teeth ached, she clenched them so tightly.

Lord Lambert's hand against the small of her back was all that propelled her forward. Left on her own, she probably would have stayed there, standing like a fool in the middle of the floor for who knew how long.

"Never you mind Down," Lord Lambert said. "He's always been a bit of an idiot."

Perhaps, but he was only voicing what every other person in the ballroom was thinking. They finally reached the balcony. It was lit with dozens of candles placed atop towering candlesticks, appearing almost like glittering stars that had dropped low to the earth. As they reached the edge of the balcony, Eliza slipped free of Lord Lambert's arm, placed both her hands on the railing, and closed her eyes. She breathed in deeply. The night air, while not downright cold, still held a nip.

Lord Lambert stood next to her, quite close. Eliza was so upset, however, she couldn't even enjoy that.

"Please tell me you are going to forget what he said," Lord Lambert pressed.

Eliza shook her head but refused to open her eyes. "It's not just him."

Lord Lambert's arm snaked around her back, holding her close to him and Eliza found herself leaning her head against his shoulder. A calm settled about her. A comfort. She, at least, was not alone.

"It doesn't seem to matter what I do, I'll never be accepted. Not truly."

"Is that so important?"

She pulled away; how could he even ask such a thing?

Lord Lambert held her gently. "You're always so quiet while in society. If you just spoke up more, I'm sure they'd all see what a brilliant, caring woman you truly are."

Eliza placed her hands against his chest, pressing back and out of his arms. "Not you, too."

"What?"

Emotion bit at her eyes, causing her sight to blur. "Ever since I've arrived in London, people have been telling me how I ought to change. That I needed to be more like this or more like that. More prim, more outspoken, more . . . something I am not." She blinked several times.

"That's not what I meant."

"But that's what you said." Her heart ached and her stomach swirled. How much longer could she tolerate this? Perhaps Rachel had been right, and they all would have been better off staying home. She certainly would have been.

"Listen to me, Eliza." Lord Lambert drew near her once more, taking her hand in his. "I'm not saying you need to change who you are."

"Don't I?" She scoffed. "My laugh is too harsh, my conversation uncouth." She squeezed his hand tighter with each statement. "I can't dance elegantly, I can't converse with ease like a young lady ought. When I do speak, it is only to say that which is most unwant-ed." With that last statement, she slammed their hands, still entwined, onto the railing. His hit below hers, taking most of the blow. She didn't miss that he winced.

Embarrassment blazed painfully against her chest. Eliza tugged her hand free of his. "Botheration," she whispered. First one, then a second, tear trailed down her cheek. She was an absolute mess. "I am sorry," she said, then turned and hurried off.

Never had she been so humiliated. More still, it wasn't as though she needed the petty nature of Lord Down or the rest of society to embarrass her, she was apparently fully capable of doing so herself.

Now Lord Lambert was fully aware of it, too.

CHAPTER SIXTEEN

Adam poked at the eggs atop his plate. She'd let him hold her. Surely that was a good sign. And she'd even been willing to open up and talk to him—something Eliza did not do with just anyone. Of course, he'd repaid her vulnerability by stumbling over his words and saying exactly the wrong thing. He'd not known his words were the wrong ones until he'd said them—blasted shame, that. If he'd been a mite bit smarter, he could have avoided the part where she pushed him away and ran off crying.

If society hadn't taken a liking to criticizing her before, seeing her shed tears at a ball had likely done her no favors. Hang it all, but she was not likely to see the end of their sharp tongues any time soon. And he was partially to blame.

Why couldn't he have said the right thing?

Adam's gaze moved over to Theodosia. Did his cousin ever feel the same as Eliza? Forever pushed to be something she wasn't? He hadn't meant that Eliza should change who she was; he'd only meant he adored the woman he was privileged to know and didn't doubt more people would as well if granted the opportunity. But he in no way wanted her to change, to be different, to be more like other women. That hadn't been it at all.

Too bad he wasn't smart enough to express such a thought politely.

He'd already arranged for flowers to be sent to her this morning. Somehow, that didn't feel like enough. He needed to see her, speak with her. Would she be at-home to visitors later today? He wasn't sure.

Kitty came into the room, nearly skipping, and took the seat directly to Adam's left. "Can you buy me more ribbons today?" she asked by way of greeting.

"Miss Kitty," Aunt Priscilla scolded from down the table, "it is impolite to ask such a thing. More still when you have not even said good morning."

"Good morning," Kitty said, the words harsh and blatantly disrespectful.

"Well," Aunt Priscilla huffed. "I hope you do not plan to let such a thing go unpunished, Adam. This girl clearly needs a firmer hand, and I think it's time you see to it."

It was too early in the morning for this.

"I said what you told me to," Kitty countered.

"Adam," Aunt Priscilla continued, "I expect you to stop her impertinence right this minute."

"Kitty, please apologize."

"Why?" Kitty's voice turned shrill. "I said what she wanted me to. Why can't I have another ribbon today?"

"Adam, this minute."

"I want a ribbon."

"This impertinence cannot continue."

"I want it!"

"You must be firm, or——"

"Enough," Adam said, slamming his hands down on the table. The sound reverberated through the room, effectively silencing both his aunt and Kitty. He had to compose himself. Adam drew in a breath, stood, and kept his voice even. "Aunt Priscilla, I have heard your recommendation. Now, if you will please excuse us, Kitty and I need to speak in the nursery."

"But I'm hungry," Kitty said, her brow low.

"I will have a plate sent up for you." He bent down, bringing himself closer to her eye level. "But you and I do need to speak now."

Her gaze dropped to the floor. "Yes, sir." Obediently, she slipped out of her chair and moved from the room.

It saddened Adam to see that she was no longer skipping. He hadn't wanted to steal the joy from her day. With his own worries over Eliza weighing him down, he wanted, now more than ever, for at least Kitty to be happy.

Adam walked out of the room, his hand on Kitty's shoulder. The moment they were out of earshot of Aunt Priscilla, with only Mr. Reid near enough to hear them, Adam spoke.

"You cannot speak to your aunt that way."

"But she's not my aunt," Kitty said, twisting about to look up at him, her tone no longer defiant.

No, with Aunt Priscilla being Adam's mother's sister, she wouldn't be Kitty's aunt. "Nonetheless," Adam said, motioning for her to continue up the stairs. "She was the sister of the late Lord Lambert, albeit only through marriage, and that makes her family."

"Not my family," she muttered.

Was she not? Or was she only being obstinate yet again? Adam glanced over at Mr. Reid.

Young though he was, the butler must have understood Adam's questioning glance, for he mouthed, "She's not."

Adam paused on the bottom step. How then *did* Kitty fit into this household? Adam had reconciled himself to the idea that she was his half-sister. It was not hard to understand why the late Lord Lambert would have concealed such a thing from a lady as prudish as Aunt Priscilla, even more so since the woman was related to the late Lord Lambert's deceased wife.

But, if Adam and Kitty did not share a father, then why the blazes was she here?

And here he'd gone and told Eliza she ought to not hide who she was; all this time, he himself had been so worried about being the man his father wished him to be, that he'd not once truly stepped up and acted as master of this house. Well, that needed to end now. Starting from this moment on, he wouldn't worry about whether he was the man his father wanted him to be or not—and he wasn't going to be afraid to look ignorant in front of his own staff. He didn't know where Kitty had come from, and surely they knew it.

It was time that changed.

If Eliza could be audacious herself, then so could he.

"Kitty," Adam said, "you go up to the nursery. I'll see you soon."

"But what about my breakfast?"

Mr. Reid stepped up. "I can bring a plate up, miss."

But Adam had something different in mind. "Send up a maid with a plate," he instructed the butler. "I want to have a word with you."

"It's about time," Mr. Reid said beneath his breath as he hurried off to see to Adam's request.

Kitty quietly climbed the stairs, but Mr. Reid was back even before she reached the next level.

"You wished to speak to me, my lord?"

"Yes, follow me." Adam moved quickly toward the library, which sat at the front of the house. He entered the space, already cleaned by maids that morning, and shut the door behind Mr. Reid. He then took a seat by the small fire and motioned for Mr. Reid to take the one opposite.

"I am sure it is no surprise to learn that my father never mentioned Miss Kitty to myself or my aunt," Adam began.

"I had thought he would have. Only, your face that first day you came . . ." Mr. Reid whistled low and then chuckled.

Adam found himself smiling. No doubt, his utter shock had been evident and probably more than a little diverting to the staff. "Well, the truth of the matter is, I still have no idea where she came from or why she's here."

Mr. Reid sobered instantly. "You're not thinking of sending her away. 'Cause if you do—"

Adam lifted a hand. "Calm down, Reid. I'm thinking nothing of the sort." Kitty was a handful, but he adored her. "I wouldn't hear of her being sent away." No matter what he learned regarding her past. "I only need to know . . ."

It was suddenly quite hard to say what he'd come to accept—or what he *believed* he had come to accept. Adam shifted about in his chair and tried again. "I need to know if she is . . . that is to say, if my father was . . ."

"If your father was hers, too?" Mr. Reid asked.

Adam nodded. Lud, this was far harder than he'd imagined it would be.

"Well, set your mind at ease. He wasn't."

"Then why take her in?" He simply could not imagine any other reason why Kitty would be living here.

"Can you not think of any reasons?"

"Only that her mother and my father . . . you know. And maybe she had Kitty *already*?"

Mr. Reid actually looked affronted. "Honestly, my lord. Can you not think of any reason your late father—a right honorable and respectable gentleman—would be taking care of another man's daughter *other* than"—he waved a hand, clearly unwilling to say the word in front of a titled man—"because he had been with her mother?"

Adam coughed, surprised at how uncomfortable he felt. To be reprimanded for thinking ill of one's own father . . . it was a strange and decidedly uneasy position. All the more so because this young butler knew Adam's own father far better than Adam ever had.

"Of all the nodcock—" Mr. Reid clamped his mouth shut, shaking his head. "He took her in out of the goodness of his heart, he did. He never knew Kitty's mum in *any* manner. None of us did." He shook his head as he looked away. "His lordship and Kitty's mum. Rubbish."

Adam felt duly reprimanded. "I'll remind you, Mr. Reid, that I do not have the advantage of knowing the character of my father. I hardly knew the man at all. You'll forgive me for being affronted that he found it so easy to spend time with someone else's child when he spent so little with his own."

Mr. Reid dropped his gaze. "Indeed, sir. My apologies."

Adam sighed. "Perhaps you should give me the whole of it so I may better understand."

Mr. Reid nodded, resting back against the chair. "It all happened several years ago. One night, I was out taking care of Lambert's horse. A man, just older than me, came up to the house, what looked like a sack of potatoes on his shoulder, he had, and asked to see Mr. George. He was the butler then. Old and gray and much more the proper butler than me. Well, George came out and, I didn't mean to eavesdrop, but there I was, and I can tell you what. He was not happy to see the man. George yelled and said he'd disowned the man long ago and wasn't about to change his mind now."

"It was George's son?"

Mr. Reid nodded. "His very own. They hadn't seen each other in over ten years, I later learned. But even all that time away, George wasn't about to mend fences."

For all the distance that had been between Adam and his own father, at least they hadn't been estranged.

"Just as George was shutting the door in the man's face, his son took the bundle off his shoulder. Only, it weren't any potatoes. It was a baby."

"Miss Kitty?" Adam asked.

"Sure thing. All tiny and wrapped up, a bit pink from the night air. It wasn't my place, but I snuck up a bit closer after seeing what he was carrying. I heard the man say that he had to leave, some bad men were after him, but more than anything he needed to know his little girl would be all right. Then he asked George to take the girl in."

Mr. Reid paused, drew in a breath, and leaned forward, resting his hands between his knees. "George was right surprised, he was. Didn't have no more words after that. He simply let his son press the little girl, his granddaughter, into his arms and then turned to leave. George stood there for a bit, and after a while, he went back inside."

"So, Miss Kitty . . . is the previous butler's granddaughter?" Surely that couldn't be the whole story. That explained why she'd come, but not why she was still here. Nor why she was currently living in the nursery, very much living the life of a daughter of a titled gentleman.

"Yes, that she is."

"Then, how did my father come to be raising the girl?"

"Well now, that happened a couple of months later. At first, George took care of the babe, with a lot of help from the maids, I can tell you. Your father, though, he was certainly generous. He let George have time off when needed, and he let the maids do all they could for the babe. Originally, we all thought Kitty's father would return after a bit. Having her around was sweet, but temporary."

"Why wasn't it?"

"After a few months, George heard rumor that his son was being hunted by smugglers. I kept my ear to the ground, and best I could gather, it was when the son first started dealing with smugglers that George disinherited him. Either way, George had a change of heart or something. He told Lord Lambert he wanted to go find his son, to save him, if possible, and bring him back. Your father not only gave George his blessing but also promised to look after Miss Kitty while he was away."

"But he never did come back, did he?"

"No, my lord," Mr. Reid said, sadly. "He never did. Your father appointed me as temporary butler while George was away. But then weeks turned into months and then into years . . . and well, here you find us now. I'm still butler, and your father kept his word. He looked after Miss Kitty as though she were his own."

"Even going so far as to buy her beaded slippers and ribbons and to secure her a governess."

"That he did. He wanted her to have every opportunity—including a good education. It was a testament to how much he adored Miss Kitty."

Gads, but that was a story. Adam turned his gaze to the low fire. The morning was warm enough that it didn't need to be large, but the small bit of heat it put off was welcome all the same. "I had no notion."

Mr. Reid only grunted.

Adam rubbed a hand over his chin. "I had rather wondered why he was raising a young girl, alone, when he had not been willing to . . ." The more he spoke, the more pitiful his sentence sounded.

"Not been willing to keep you?" Mr. Reid finished for him.

It sounded ever more pitiful when someone else said it. Still, Adam nodded.

"I wasn't around when your mum passed," Mr. Reid said, his tone turning thoughtful. "He didn't speak of her often. But the few times I did hear him talk of her, it was always with a deep sadness, a longing. I don't know that he ever got over her, not really."

It did Adam's heart much good to hear it. For months now, he'd been under the impression that his father had been more than over his mother—over her and moved on.

"Did he ever . . ." Adam drew in a breath, but he'd already shown himself to be both ignorant and pitiful. No reason to stop now. "Did he ever mention me?"

"Now and then."

"No more than that?"

"I'm sorry, my lord." Mr. Reid stood, slowly making his way toward the door. "I'm just a simple man, you know. I wouldn't presume to understand a man as great as your father."

"But?" Adam encouraged.

"The few times I *did* hear him speak of you, it was with a similar love and longing as when he spoke of your mother. Now, I may be wrong, but I always believed that he took Miss Kitty in, in part, to make up for not having raised you. I think he hoped it would redeem him, in a way."

Staring at the fire, the image Adam had of his father shifted yet again. Like it had so many times since coming to London, what he had believed blurred like a painting beneath water. Blurred and changed and then, for the first time ever, it settled.

The shadows stopped their shifting, the lines pulled straight. The few facts Adam knew of the man who'd been his father came together.

Adam could see the late Lord Lambert, young and in love. Then heartbroken and distraught over the loss of his sweetheart. What else could a man, suddenly alone in the world, do? He would have listened to his friends and neighbors—let the mother's family raise the boy, they'd have said.

Adam could see the late Lord Lambert, struggling to come to terms with all that had happened, not wanting to visit. Not wanting to be forced to look at a growing boy, only to face all he'd lost.

Writing would have been easier.

Adam could see the late Lord Lambert, capitulating when his butler asked simply for a bit of time and help in raising a grand-daughter, one he'd not even known he'd had before that night. The late Lord Lambert would have looked at the small babe, remembered his own and how he regretted not raising his son himself. He would have agreed. Miss Kitty would have been a welcome addition to the home.

Adam could see his father, helping his butler—a man close in age to himself—deal with the tiny infant. Then, his father would have certainly agreed to care for the girl while the butler left to find his son. And when George didn't return? What else was he to do besides continue as he had been?

Adam could see his father raising Kitty as his own. Not because he hadn't wanted Adam, or because he loved Kitty more than he'd loved Adam. But because by then, he'd simply been wiser. He'd known what it meant to give up a baby and he knew better than to do it again.

"He had nothing to redeem for," Adam said. He'd had a good life. Aunt Priscilla, for all her sternness, had been a good mother to him. "But I thank you all the same, Reid."

Adam turned toward where the young butler had been standing near the door. Only, he wasn't there anymore. Adam was alone in the room.

He stood slowly. Now that he knew Kitty's history and who she was, he felt better able to handle her—to raise her himself. Knowing more about his father was also a boon. There was a peace inside him he'd been lacking for years.

Adam left the room and silently walked up the stairs.

Kitty was not playing with her doll or sitting at her small table eating, as he had imagined she would be. Instead, she was sitting atop the window bench, staring out at the clouds.

Wordless, he moved toward her, sitting down on the little spot of the bench she didn't take up.

"You thought we were family," she stated.

"I had wondered if we weren't."

"Now that you know we're not, are you going to send me away?"

It made sense now why the entire household both expected him to do as much when he'd first arrived and was equally adamant he not. A titled gentleman did not raise a butler's granddaughter. At the same time, this little girl belonged to a man who'd served the family for years, and had no doubt been highly respected; she was the little girl their master had agreed to take care of until the butler returned, which now, would probably never happen.

"No," Adam said at length. "I'll not be sending you away."

Kitty let out something like a hiccup and then flung herself at him, wrapping her arms around his middle and pressing her face against him. "I'm sorry I was mean to your aunt."

"Oh, sweetie," he said, rubbing her back, "that's all right. But I do hope you understand you must speak respectfully to others. You are a good, kind girl and I expect nothing less from you."

"I know," she said, her voice muffled by the fabric of his jacket. "I'll do better."

"You will need to apologize, you know."

"Yes," she said, still not letting go. "I promise I will."

"Then dry your tears." He kept rubbing her back. He'd never dreamed of arriving in London to find a ward for him to care for; yet now, he wouldn't wish it any other way. "This is your home, and we'll just keep looking after one another."

She squeezed him tightly. "I love you, Adam."

He smiled and even had to blink a couple of times. "And I, you, Kitty."

CHAPTER SEVENTEEN

E liza smoothed her dress yet again. After running away from Lord Lambert last night, she'd half expected him to come call today.

Perhaps that was foolish of her?

After all, it wasn't as though he were actually courting her.

But he had held her so very tenderly. Good heavens, but the memory alone caused her heart to race and her face to heat and her hands to become jittery. It was a wonder no one had asked her about it yet this morning.

Rachel was once more overwrought at the lack of response from her mother and Dinah seemed in a bit of a snit, though Eliza wasn't sure why. Lady Blackmore sat directly beside Eliza, but even she seemed strangely despondent. No one, apparently, was their right self today.

"Mr. Collin," the footman announced, leading the man himself into the room.

"Good day to you all," he said easily enough. Still, the simple greeting alone felt too cheerful for the mood they were all in. It hit the room, garish in comparison, and fell to the floor, unheeded.

Was it his usual calling day already? Eliza had not realized an entire week had passed since last he'd come. Still, she motioned toward the chair to her left.

"How do you find yourself today?" she asked. After all, someone needed to make conversation, and it was up to her, as the eldest, to see such things taken care of.

"Quite well, thank you. And yourselves?"

Eliza glanced about her. Rachel kept her gaze on the hands in her lap, Dinah was scowling at nothing in particular, and Lady Blackmore's face was angled toward the large window.

"We are all well," Eliza lied.

"I can see." Mr. Collin looked from her to the other women in the room, not sounding the least bit convinced. He leaned forward, resting an arm against his knee. "Would you care to take a turn about the room with me?"

What Eliza wanted was a chance to get away from the drama filling the house. A turn about the room just wouldn't be enough. "Suppose we took a turn outside?"

"A stroll seems just the thing," Mr. Collin agreed, standing.

Eliza followed him out of the room, gathered her pelisse and bonnet, and then they slipped from the house. Neither Rachel nor Lady Blackmore so much as spoke up at their leaving. Dinah didn't even blink, which surprised Eliza the most. After all, if anyone hated to be left out of any social foray—even be it so small as a turn down the street—it was Dinah.

"I have to admit," Mr. Collin said, pointing a finger back over his shoulder and toward the house they'd just left, "that is one thing I don't miss about home."

Eliza wished she could laugh but found she couldn't. "Rachel's mood I understand. Lady Blackmore's isn't hard to guess at. But I have no idea what's bothering Dinah."

Mr. Collin shrugged. "Whatever it may be, I'm sure it'll pass soon enough. Young women are forever finding themselves distraught over something."

Eliza looked at him askance. "I am not so very much older than Dinah. Am I also one of those young women who are forever finding themselves distraught?"

Mr. Collin shook his head. "You've far too much common sense for such a thing."

Eliza could not remember a time when a compliment sounded so similar to an insult.

"At least," he said, slowing his walk, "there was a time when you were quite sensible."

This compliment just kept improving. "And am I not now?"

"I seem to recall some rather ill-advised words spoken to Lady Oakley not long ago."

Ah, that. The nightmare that wouldn't let her sleep. "If you are still wishing I show some regret, I am afraid you have come for naught."

"Eliza." He stopped, placing a hand on her arm to halt her. "Surely you must realize how unwise that was. You cannot go about gainsaying a woman of the *haut ton*. Understand"—he started them walking once more—"when I first learned of your situation, I was not so very worried for you. Your sister, yes. Even your cousin. But not you. You're quiet and unassuming. You're exactly the type of woman society *wants* you to be."

His words made her want to wriggle, as a bee crawling down one's back did.

"You've been granted an opportunity to socialize with them, but that doesn't mean they'll see you as an equal. Trust me. So long as you play their game, they'll let you stay. But continue as you did, and your father's title won't mean anything. You'll be in every black book in Town."

"Play their game?" She couldn't keep all the indignation out of her voice. "And how exactly do you propose I do that?"

If he heard the hurt in her tone, he didn't show it. "Be submissive. Be agreeable. Compliment and flatter them. Marry someone from your station, then slip back out of their lives and back to the country."

"Excuse me?"

"This is a thrilling adventure, I'll grant you. But no one actually believes you're here to stay."

The sting of before sunk deeper. Perhaps he was right. Though

Eliza, Dinah, and Rachel had all enjoyed attention while here in Town, not a single gentleman had actually taken up an acquaintance with them in earnest. The women they met talked about them, around them, above them, but never truly *to* them. She hated thinking Mr. Collin was correct, but the more she thought on it, the more she could only find evidence that he was. They turned in their walk, and the house once more stood in front of them instead of behind. For several minutes, they simply walked in silence.

They had been quiet in one another's company before, but not in such a way as this. This time, it felt awkward, unsettling. The house Father was letting grew larger as they approached; a reminder that this small reprieve from all that was inside would soon be over.

But which Eliza would return? The quiet, submissive one Mr. Collin saw her to be? The openly flirty young woman Rachel and Dinah seemed to wish she was? Neither sat well with her.

"Eliza." Mr. Collin took her hand in his as they reached the steps to the house. "I did have something particular I wished to say to you."

"Oh?"

"I will be in London for two weeks more. When I leave, I will only be going as far as the southern border and will be sure to leave word with your butler on how you may reach me."

"That is very good of you." If also a bit unusual—he seemed to be saying something more than just the words he uttered, but she couldn't piece together what exactly.

He must have seen the confusion on her face, for he patted the hand inside his own with his other. "My dear, if you reach the end of your Season, or if you reach the end of your patience with society, all you need do is let me know."

She nodded, but only to convey she was listening; she didn't actually know where he was going with this.

"I may only be a simple, untitled man, but I *have* risen to boatswain. I associate with many gentlemen of the *ton*. Why, the men you saw me with the night we first met, one is the second son of a baron and another the fourth son of an earl. A connection between us would not be unseemly for either of our families."

A connection? "Are you proposing, then?"

He listed his head. "Of course. After all, what could be a better fit than you and me? More still, though I do associate with many well-connected gentlemen, you can be assured that you won't be forced into company with so high members of the peerage as Lady Oakley. A relief to you, no doubt."

"No doubt," she echoed.

Marry Mr. Collin? The idea caused her to still, to go numb, actually. She found the idea neither repulsive nor intriguing.

It was simply . . . an option.

Shouldn't a marriage proposal elicit more emotion than that, though?

"I must bid you good day, my dear," he said. Was it only her, or was there no more affection in his tone than there had been before? No slightly hidden yearning, no closely guarded passion. Only cordiality. "As I said, only let me know when you wish to have the wedding date set. I am in no rush as there are no plans for me to leave the continent."

Without waiting for her to reply, he turned and strode away.

Dumbfounded, Eliza climbed the steps then turned and watched him leave.

Her mind flitted back to when they'd both been young, before he'd gone to sea, before she'd become the daughter of a knight. She'd once or twice allowed herself to daydream of what it might be like to receive a marriage proposal from Mr. Collin. Never in her mind, though, had it played out as the actual proposal had on the street below.

Nonetheless, what more could she expect? Mr. Collin had been correct in his assessment that no gentleman in Town truly wanted a connection with her family. But what of Lord Lambert? As much as she wished—desperately so—that he would show pointed interest in her, he hadn't. All the emotions she believed ought to be present during a proposal flooded through her. The way Lord Lambert had held her last night still echoed across her skin. How she longed to be held like that again.

Then she'd gone and ruined it all by running away from him. No doubt, such addresses would not be renewed.

Eliza turned toward the door as the butler opened it. She took a step forward but paused just before the threshold. She peered up at the house's facade. It looked exactly the same as every other house along this street. Yet, inside, it held a family unlike anything London had ever known before. Was there a place among society for her and her family?

Shaking her head, she finally stepped inside.

No, for a family such as hers, there certainly wasn't.

CHAPTER EIGHTEEN

E liza tried to relax—she truly did. But sitting directly beside Augusta, with Lord Lambert across from them in the open-top barouche, was not relaxing.

Neither she nor Lord Lambert mentioned the last time they'd spoken, the time she'd become an emotional wreck and then stormed off. What must he think of her now? He must not hate her, at least, for he'd seemed quite happy to have her join him and Augusta today. That was something at least, but she still wasn't confident he didn't think less of her now.

It was ridiculous—nonsense, Father would say—but she couldn't be at ease.

More still, Mr. Collin's words from yesterday had not stopped ringing in her mind. What would her life be like if she accepted him? If she didn't, would she not be denying herself a comfortable life for one where she never truly fit in, was never fully accepted?

She hazarded a glance at Lord Lambert. His eyes met hers and he smiled—it was *that* smile. The one he'd worn the night they'd dined at his home. The one that seemed to speak of something more than friendship. The one that made her heart skip.

Was he not put out with her, though? If the smile had been

confusing before, now it was distressingly so. She couldn't seem to puzzle out what he was thinking. Did Lord Lambert not see that she would never belong in his world? Eliza felt her throat thicken with emotion. It was all very troubling, indeed.

This was Mr. Collin's fault, really.

He'd put ideas in her head, and now she couldn't shake them loose.

She did not belong, but she was beginning to fear that neither could she return to what had been.

The comfort that the three of them had enjoyed these past many weeks felt horribly unattainable now.

"This is lovely, is it not?" Augusta asked, her gaze traveling over the full length of the park.

The trees were full of flowers, and the grass was green once more. Several other carriages were out, and Augusta nodded frequently to those they passed. Eliza smiled softly at the sight.

"Yes, it is," she agreed. Though she'd always loved the spring, this time the joy at seeing the seasons change was bittersweet. She was glad for the warmth, but not the least bit confident the summer would bring pleasant times.

Augusta placed her hand atop Eliza's. "This is proving every bit as wondrous as I always dreamed it would be. Oh, look, I do believe that's Lord Fitzwilliam just ahead. I had not heard he'd come for the Season." She lifted a hand, giving the gentleman a dainty wave of her fingers. He saw her, smiled, and turned his horse in their direction. As he made his way toward them, Augusta dropped her voice low and whispered, "His country seat is not half a day's journey from Town and I understand he and his Grandmother, the Dowager Fitzwilliam, are forever popping back and forth. A week in the country, a couple of weeks in town, a month in the country, a few days here. Back and forth, all Season long."

She had to leave off then, for the gentleman was upon them. He wore a most refined jacket of dark blue, and his hat was the tallest Eliza had ever seen. It rested jauntily atop a head of shocking blond hair—so light, in fact, it nearly looked white.

"Lord Fitzwilliam," Augusta said, her smile brightening. "It has been far too long since last we saw one another."

"Far too long indeed," Lord Fitzwilliam said, his gaze not staying on Augusta long. Instead, it roved from her to Eliza, to Lord Lambert, and back to Eliza. "Pardon me," he said, eyes on Eliza, "but I do not believe I've had the pleasure."

Introductions were quickly made after which Augusta asked after Lord Fitzwilliam's grandmother.

"I hope she will be quite well again soon, though at the moment she has something of a fever."

That was too bad, but Eliza was having a hard time focusing on Lord Fitzwilliam, for she could feel Lord Lambert watching her intently. Had her bonnet gone askew?

"It's not serious, I hope," Augusta said.

Eliza glanced over at Lord Lambert. He didn't seem concerned with how she looked, he simply seemed to be watching her.

"Who knows with Grandmother," Lord Fitzwilliam said. "Either way, she has sent me to Town to find for her a bit of canary yellow ribbon. She claims the sight of a new yellow ribbon always cures what ails her. Though I confess I haven't the first notion where to find such a thing."

"Three streets over," Lord Lambert said, pointing past them all. "There's a small shop on the corner. Quite the largest selection of ribbons I've ever seen."

Had he been buying more for Miss Kitty? The young girl clearly adored the few ribbons Lord Lambert had purchased her previously.

"I'm much obliged to you," Lord Fitzwilliam said, already angling his horse that way. "Good day to you all."

They called their farewells, but most likely he was already too far away to hear.

"Isn't he most singular?" Augusta said, her nose wrinkling. "His whole *household* is quite peculiar."

"He did seem quite bent on finding the right ribbon," Eliza agreed. Though she hadn't spoken to Lord Fitzwilliam directly, he had seemed a genuine enough man.

"And so handsome," Augusta said, waggling her eyebrows and then giggling. "Did you not think so, Eliza?"

Lord Lambert's gaze snapped back toward her. Eliza felt her face warm, though she fought it valiantly. What did Augusta mean by putting her on the spot like this? Asking if she found one gentleman attractive while sitting across from the very one her heart longed for—it was quite distressing.

Nonetheless, hadn't Lord Lambert said she ought to be audacious more often? If he felt so certain on that point, perhaps he'd like a taste of what he was asking of her.

"I did find him quite handsome," Eliza said. "Truly, who would not with hair the color of his?"

"Dramatic, isn't it?" Augusta agreed.

"Quite."

For his part, Lord Lambert remained silent. But Eliza could sense him tensing from across the carriage.

It was a strange sort of satisfaction to think that perhaps Lord Lambert was not wholly unfeeling toward her preferences. Perhaps being audacious had its benefits.

"Still," Eliza said, not looking directly at Lord Lambert, but allowing her gaze to move about those passing them in the park, "I feel certain he and I will never be more than passing acquaintances."

"Oh?" Augusta asked.

Lord Lambert seemed equally interested in her answer.

"I don't believe I could ever truly prefer a man who bought a woman ribbon when she was ill with fever."

Augusta laughed. "Lady Blackmore knows the Dowager Fitzwilliam quite well, and she will attest that in *that* house, buying ribbons to bring an end to their fever is quite as normal as everything else they do."

What a house that must be. "And to think," Eliza said, "society struggles to accept me simply because I do my own sister's hair from time to time."

Even Lord Lambert laughed at that.

"Society is not exactly known for its common sense," Augusta added, waving yet another gentleman acquaintance over.

⁂

Adam stayed silent for most of the ride through Hyde Park. Lady Augusta had not assumed wrong when she thought she might enjoy a ride at the fashionable hour. It seemed Lady Augusta was overjoyed with all the acquaintances they chanced to meet. For himself, he enjoyed the warm early spring air. More than once, he caught Eliza eying not the gentlemen who passed them by but their horses.

The sight brought him immense pleasure. He would dearly love to show her the many horses in his father's stable at his Northernmost seat. There were acres and acres of perfect riding terrain, too. Flat enough not to be too strenuous on the horse, not too wooded to be difficult to wind one's way through, but still open and untamed. She would love it.

Now, the only problem left was how to go about it.

He'd been trying for some time now to ascertain for himself how she felt about him. They were friends, that much he knew. But could she ever see her way to them becoming *more* than friends? To them forming a more permanent connection? Eliza's naturally quiet demeanor never bothered him; he quite enjoyed the calm that seemed to be forever about her, but it did make her thoughts rather difficult to ascertain at times.

By the time the driver brought them back to Lady Augusta's home, Adam was no closer to knowing how Eliza felt toward him.

He stepped down and handed both ladies out.

Lady Augusta thanked him profusely.

Eliza, on the other hand, was more subdued in her gratitude. Was that because she was pleased with their ride but not overly so? When their eyes met, he could have sworn he wasn't the only one who felt the sparks.

Either that, or he was a complete coxcomb and reading things into their interactions that weren't there at all.

At least both women promised him a dance at Almack's the next evening.

It was a very long twenty-four hours.

So long, in fact, that he even went so far as to seek out Theodosia's advice on which jacket he ought to wear. He knew enough of his own preference to know he was more likely to offend a woman if he chose his own clothing than to successfully woo her.

Almack's was quite full to the brim. The gathering was probably close to double what it had been that fateful night he'd tripped over Eliza's slippered feet. Did she think back on that night as often as he did?

He tugged on the hem of the sleeves of his jacket—a midnight blue superfine—and strode into the room. His aunt had chosen to remain home tonight, which left him alone to find Eliza. He was through putting off telling her how he felt. Even just between the time he first realized he cared for her until now, he'd gone from hoping she'd allow him to call on her to hoping she'd accept his offer.

Not that he *was* going to offer for her tonight. He'd no doubt scare her away.

But, surely if he danced with her a couple of times, spoke with her during several other dances, and asked to call on her next week, she'd understand his intentions.

His heart sped up at the thought. Clenching his hands into tight fists, he pushed deeper into the room. He couldn't do anything until he found her, and in the swarm that had descended on Almack's tonight, it wasn't going to be easy. Two sets had begun and ended before the crowd parted on his left and, between a well-togged man and an elderly matron, he spied Eliza.

She stood beside her sister, her cousin, and Lady Blackmore. They seemed to be talking earnestly with one another—or rather, Eliza, Miss Dinah, and Miss Chant were earnestly speaking to Lady Blackmore who appeared more eager to ignore what was being said than face any of the three young women.

Adam pushed through the crowd. Were they having some kind of argument? He hoped not. He'd come to know Lady Blackmore well enough during all the times she'd been with Eliza. She'd always struck him as a kind-hearted woman.

He reached them just in time to hear Miss Chant say, "But the way things are between you two cannot continue."

"Lord Lambert," Lady Blackmore said loudly enough to silence any other comments from the young women. "It is good to see you this evening."

He bowed. "The pleasure is all mine."

"Tell us," Miss Dinah said before he could say more, "do you find that friendship ends after a single argument?"

His brow lifted. Her question had been as sudden as it had been unexpected. Were they talking of his argument with Eliza? He glanced over at her, but she was giving her sister a flat stare and not looking at him at all. Had she told her family of the nodcock things he'd said?

"Come now, Dinah," Lady Blackmore said, "I'm sure Lord Lambert would agree that friendship doesn't end after a single argument. *I'm* not saying it does either. It's often not the argument itself that is the problem, but the issues hiding behind it."

"Well *I'm* sure," Miss Dinah pressed, "that his lordship would agree that even the issues hiding behind an argument can be resolved."

Though they kept speaking of him, no one was looking at Adam; instead, all eyes rested on the dowager. Were they speaking of him and Eliza? Or someone else entirely? He was quite confused.

"Some issues run deep," Lady Blackmore said, not meeting anyone's gaze but instead shaking her head. "Some people are just too different."

Now, he felt fairly certain this truly had nothing to do with him. But he had no more notion who was the subject of the conversation.

"You, yourself, said the opposite when we first arrived," Miss Chant said.

Adam leaned in close to Eliza and spoke softly so only she might hear. "Of whom are we speaking?"

She placed a hand on his arm, leaning in yet closer. Her nearness spread a heated awareness coursing over his skin. The ache to wrap his arm around her and pull her still nearer was nearly over-powering.

"Lady Blackmore and my father have quarreled," she whispered.

"I see."

She pulled away, even while speaking to the other women. "You said you both needed time to calm down, but it has been time enough already. Surely now you two might make amends?"

He wished she'd lean back toward him. He no doubt ought to be thinking over Lady Blackmore and Sir Mulgrave's disagreement and help them find a solution—for he truly did believe that friends ought not argue and stay apart—but, just now, all he could think about was how heavenly it would be to dance with Eliza and have an excuse for her to be near him once more.

"I do not know if he even cares for us to make amends," Lady Blackmore said, her voice a bit softer than before.

"I know he does," Eliza said, moving over toward her. "He has not been himself any more than you have since the argument."

Lady Blackmore gave her a half-smile. "Then perhaps I might speak with him tomorrow. Now," she turned toward Adam, "I'm sure this gentleman did not come over here to learn of my paltry problems."

"I only wished to ask Miss Mulgrave if she would join me for the next set, my lady."

Lady Blackmore turned toward Eliza, who smiled her agreement.

Though Eliza had agreed to dance with him the last time they had both attended a ball, it still made his chest warm to see her looking so obviously pleased by the invitation.

He extended his elbow and she accepted it, but he didn't wait until they were more than two steps away before speaking.

"And while we're on the topic of friends and arguments, I do hope this means you've forgiven me for the other day."

Eliza was silent for a minute—a long minute. Did that mean she hadn't truly forgiven him?

At length, she spoke. "I must admit, I was rather hurt by your words at the time."

"My meaning was unclear, I fear," he said. "Might you forgive me?"

"That depends," she said as he led her to the spot where they would begin the dance. "What did you actually mean?"

He was forced to leave her side then; the music was starting and the dance required they start facing one another but not so near to actually speak privately.

The first notes filled the air and Eliza and the man directly to Adam's left turned about one another. He then did the same with the woman on Eliza's right. Blessedly, only a few measures later, he was allowed to take Eliza's hand and walk a few steps with her.

"Only this." He spoke quickly; they would not have much time together. "That you are magnificent, and those who think otherwise are unequivocally wrong."

That was all the time they had before they separated. It was several lines of music before they again walked side by side and were able to speak and not be overheard.

"I don't want you to change," Adam said, his voice low and rushed. "I'd never ask that of you. When I said you ought to be audacious more often, I meant you ought to be audaciously *you* more often."

They parted again, but he thought there was a smile across her lips as Eliza walked away. At least, that's what he hoped he'd caught sight of. They circled about and came face to face. Though she was all that was demure, her eyes sparkled. They didn't speak while standing across from one another. At least on Adam's part, it was because he had nothing to say that he wished overheard, and his mind was too full of those private things he wanted to speak to allow room for anything else.

Finally, they moved close enough to speak. "I'm saying," Adam whispered, "that no matter who's present, no matter what anyone else will think, no matter what's happening, I hope you can be you, be brave enough to *stay* you, regardless."

They had to separate, but for only a few measures. Then, for the last time, they stood side by side.

"That you have the audacity to be yourself, no matter who else is around, is one of the reasons you have become so dear to me."

She sucked in a breath but kept her head down as she turned and moved away from him.

The dance forced them to circle around and end facing one another. Though Eliza bowed, she didn't look up.

Had he gone too far? Said the wrong thing? Said the right thing too soon?

He moved up to Eliza, extending his elbow. She slipped her hand around it and they walked away from the dance floor. He didn't take her back to where Miss Chant and Lady Blackmore were sitting. It seemed Miss Dinah had joined their dance and hadn't yet made it back. That Adam hadn't noticed her once as they flowed by every other couple on the dance floor was a testament to how truly enchanting Eliza was.

Adam moved toward a far wall, where there was more space to breathe and less of a chance they'd be overheard.

"I do think I understand what you meant," Eliza said.

Adam breathed out some relief. "So you forgive me?"

"Most certainly. I'm only sorry I ran off like I did."

He took her hand. "Think nothing of it." Even with them both wearing gloves, the touch of her hand was intoxicating. She was so very lovely tonight, her gown an alluring cut and her eyes the deepest of browns.

"But I do want you to know that I understand," she continued. "I'm just not sure the person you *think* I could be is someone I actually can be."

"You're already her."

Eliza's cheeks pinked. "I'm not sure about that. For instance, just now, if I were that audacious woman you think I am, I wouldn't be standing here talking to you."

Not exactly what he was hoping for. "You wouldn't?"

She glanced past him. "No, I'd be over *there*, pulling Dinah away from Lord Down."

Adam turned and looked over his shoulder. "I somehow never saw one of the Mulgrave women falling for a man like him."

"You mean a self-important cad, an uncivil jackanapes?"

Adam smiled at her sincerity.

She caught sight of his smile and only shook her head. "I suppose a true woman of society would never have used such words."

"You can keep trying to deny it, but you, my dear, are audacious through and through."

That, at least, brought a small smile to her lips. Her soft, pink, inviting lips. "He called on her yesterday, and would you believe it, she entertained his company for a full quarter of an hour? I'm truly beginning to worry for her."

It was blasted nice to be speaking with Eliza once more. Yes, they'd spoken while out riding through Hyde Park, but not like this.

This was just the two of them, telling secrets and standing so close they just might start rumors.

But he wanted more than just secrets and rumors.

"Would you do me a favor?" he asked.

Eliza's gaze left her sister and landed on him. Lud, but he adored those large brown eyes.

"Would you . . ." he started, suddenly more nervous than he'd thought he would be. "Would you permit me to call on you? Perhaps entertain *my* company for a quarter of an hour?"

She listed her head, her brow dropping in puzzlement. "Lord Lambert, you call on us quite frequently as it is."

"Perhaps." He reached a hand out toward a small lock of hair which tumbled across her shoulder—would she flinch at the touch? —and brushed it back behind her. "But what if I called on *you*?"

Far from flinching, she seemed to still at his touch, her gaze jumped to his lips and back up. Heat pulsed across his skin.

Leaning down, he whispered, "And you should call me Adam."

She didn't pull back but tipped her head up ever so slightly. "Adam?"

"Yes, dearest." Their noses were nearly touching. In the back of his mind, he realized that standing so close to her with hundreds of people around them was courting danger. But the voice never grew loud enough to truly bother him. More still, he had to focus on not leaning in the rest of the way, on not pressing his lips against hers. He didn't have enough energy to do that *and* listen to the voice of warning.

"Then perhaps you might call me Eliza?" she said.

"Eliza." He'd thought the name so many times but had never had permission to use it before. It flowed off his tongue like it was always meant to be spoken by him.

"Eliza!" A woman behind her called out. "There you are!"

Eliza pulled away from him, turning toward the sound.

Adam righted himself. His head swam and his heart was pounding furiously. He gave the couples around them a quick glance. Blessedly, no one seemed to be paying them the least bit of attention. Now that he had a bit of space between himself and Eliza, he realized how blasted close he had come to doing something that might have caused her grief.

He ought to thank whoever had come and stopped him in time; truly, he ought to have listened to the voice of warning a bit harder.

Lady Augusta hurried toward them. Adam wasn't surprised to see her, more surprised that he hadn't seen her already.

"Oh, Eliza," Augusta said. It wasn't a greeting of merriment, but one of distress. "Please, I must speak with you. Lord Lambert . . . good evening to you." She curtsied hurriedly. "I did not see you." She turned directly back to Eliza. "Please, there is so much I must tell you."

If she hadn't noticed him until she had already spoken several sentences to Eliza, then Lady Augusta must truly be distraught.

Eliza glanced over at him, seeming to ask if he minded that she leave. "Never mind me," he said, placing a hand at the small of her back. "Go comfort your friend."

She repaid him with a smile that made his chest heat once more and made him wish he had every right to bend down and kiss her. Instead, however, he simply whispered, "We can talk more later."

"Thank you," Eliza said. She took Lady Augusta's arm and began walking away.

Both women had only taken a couple of steps, however, when Lady Augusta pulled to a stop and looked back at him. "You did promise me a dance this evening, my lord. I do hope you mean to collect soon." Then she batted her lashes.

Adam only watched after her, dumbfounded. Lady Augusta had never once batted her lashes at him. And the way she smiled at him?

It wasn't her usual, carefree smile. It was something far more practiced, even fake.

Finally, both women were swallowed up in the crush, leaving Adam fully alone. He shook his head and moved toward the refreshment table. Hopefully, whatever Lady Augusta needed to tell Eliza wouldn't take long. He already missed having her by his side.

Still, no matter how joyful he was feeling over deepening his connection with Eliza, the look in Lady Augusta's eye as she left wormed its way into his hope and left him feeling less confident and more ill at ease.

CHAPTER NINETEEN

The way Augusta nearly pulled Eliza's arm from her shoulder could not be a good sign.

Nonetheless, Eliza's mind kept jumping back to Adam. How she longed to be back with him, standing near him, close enough she could smell the sandalwood soap on him. Her stomach fluttered happily at the thought.

Augusta yanked particularly hard, forcing Eliza to focus on the moment, else she would surely trip and end up splayed across the dance floor. Hopefully, this would not take long.

But one look at Augusta's pale face told her otherwise. Finally, they reached the doors to the ballroom and slipped through them. The hallway was not nearly as crowded, and most of the individuals were more focused on entering than on two young women who needed a bit of privacy.

Augusta finally came to a stop several paces away from the door.

"What is it?" Eliza asked, refusing to rub her shoulder despite the ache there.

"Oh, it is terrible."

Eliza's stomach fell clear to her feet. "Tell me at once." Eliza eyed her friend up and down, but she looked quite well-turned out. All excepting her red eyes. "Are you ill? Hurt?"

Augusta shook her head vehemently

That, at least, was a relief. "Is it your mother? Your father?"

More shaking of her head, which sent Augusta's perfectly set blonde curls bouncing back and forth until one came loose from its pin. "No. No, it is much worse."

Eliza placed her hands on either of Augusta's shoulders. She could feel her friend shaking. If it wasn't for either of her parents, Eliza could only think of one other. "Your sister?"

"Oh!" Augusta collapsed.

Eliza stepped forward, wrapping Augusta in her arms and easing her down into a chair. Eliza sat on the floor beside her friend, her hand on Augusta's knee, as she often did with her sisters. It had always seemed to calm them. Hopefully, it would do the same for her friend.

"Tell me all about it," Eliza said softly.

Augusta cried for several minutes before she could manage to speak. But, at length, she did. "A message came this afternoon. I thought it must mean Jane was well enough to finally come join us. I told you she was too ill to travel before, didn't I?"

Eliza nodded. They'd discussed Jane so many times Eliza felt she already knew the woman.

"Well, it was from Jane. Only, it wasn't to say she would be joining us."

"She hasn't turned for the worst, has she?" No one in the family had believed Jane's ailment was the least bit serious, only inconvenient as it had come on right as the family had planned to leave for Town. But suppose they'd been wrong?

"Oh, no." Augusta sniffled, then pulled herself up. "She confessed. She's never had been sick at all."

Eliza's brow dropped. What did Jane mean by saying she'd been ill if she hadn't been?

"It was a ruse all along. In actuality, Jane had wanted to stay behind because . . ." Augusta took in a breath and spoke softer. "Because there was a man."

"Oh, my." Eliza spoke without meaning to.

Augusta nodded her agreement. "He is an undergardener of our father's estate. She knew such a relationship would be forbidden, and so she kept it hidden. And now—" A sob broke free.

Eliza patted her softly, letting her friend know she had support.

Augusta closed her eyes. "And now they have gone to Gretna Green."

Eliza hated to see her friend so distraught. Surely, though, taking a moment to look on the bright side might help. "It might not be so bad," Eliza tried. "If he truly loves her and she, him, then at least they'll be happy."

Augusta's eyes popped open, and she stared down at Eliza, aghast. "You cannot be serious. He's an *undergardener*."

"It's true she will not know the comfort she had growing up. But that doesn't mean she won't be—"

"What? Happy?" The words came out harsh and loud. "Is that all there is in life? One's own happiness?"

Eliza reeled back, surprised. She'd never seen Augusta so angry.

"What of family?" Augusta continued. "What of responsibility?"

"Perhaps you should wait until you see your sister next. Then talk to her honestly."

Augusta huffed. "That's easy for you to say. Your father was in trade a year ago. Of course being married to an undergardener is no great shock. But for someone of my birth . . ."

Of all the people to throw her upbringing back in her face, Eliza had never expected it of Augusta. Eliza's lips pinched and she withdrew her hand from her friend's lap. Slowly, she stood.

"Oh, Eliza." Augusta's tone turned soft, penitent even. "Don't you see? This will *ruin* me. Once it is known what my sister has done, I will be the laughing stock of society. No gentleman will see me as an eligible choice."

It hadn't been Eliza's first thought—she'd been more focused on the fact that Jane had found someone whom she loved and who loved her back. But what Augusta said was true.

Augusta stood and moved closer to Eliza. "I have a couple of weeks, Father believes. If we're lucky, as much as a month, before everyone knows. I must find myself a husband before then."

"Augusta, that's terribly fast. How can you be sure of a man's character, his nature, after so short an acquaintance?" Eliza's own Father was at least giving her the entire Season. Even that felt like a frightfully short amount of time. But to secure a man in only two weeks' time? That was beyond daunting.

"I must," Augusta said, lifting her chin. "It is either that or find my own undergardener." She ground the last couple of words out.

Eliza wanted to argue. If a man was honorable, what did his station in life matter? But Augusta was hurt and reeling. Eliza could show some compassion and let the sentiment lie.

"Well, there is Lord Tulk. He has called on you a few times, I believe." Augusta had never been one to sit out many dances while at a ball or entertain during her at-homes to an empty room. "Mr. Powell has shown you a good bit of preference, I believe."

Augusta shook her head. "I have thought of them all. There is only one man who will do, I am certain. But I may need your help if I am to secure him so quickly."

"Of course." Eliza would do anything for her friend. Provided the man was good to her.

"It must be Lord Lambert."

Eliza's entire body went cold.

"We have all spent quite a bit of time together," Augusta continued. "While I am not certain he holds any preference for me, I feel he *might* if only I encourage him a bit."

Lord Lambert? No, Eliza couldn't help with that.

Then again, Eliza had never once mentioned her own preference to her friend, and she had always suspected Augusta was oblivious to it. Now she was quite certain.

But did she dare say anything? It seemed silly when there was nothing officially settled between her and Lord Lambert.

What did they have between them? An agreement to use one another's Christian names, and that was all.

"Eliza?" Augusta asked. "Are you all right?"

Eliza nodded but couldn't yet find words.

"You don't think Lord Lambert would be opposed to the idea, do you?"

Yes, she did. That was to mean, she *hoped* he would be.

Either way, Eliza couldn't stay silent. "I had rather the impression . . ." This was immensely hard to say. "I mean, I had thought his preferences leaned elsewhere." She gave Augusta an apologetic smile.

Augusta's brow creased. "Did you? I had rather the impression he was spending time with us to avoid all of society, as much as anything."

"Perhaps at first," Eliza tried again. "But now——"

Augusta reached out and took a firm hold of Eliza's arm. Light seemed to dawn in her eyes. Eliza felt both relieved and a bit anxious. She'd never so much as breathed a word of hope that she and Lord Lambert would further their connection to anyone, not even Rachel or Dinah. Still, it felt wonderful to express such hope to her friend at last.

"Don't tell me," Augusta said, but there was no joy in her tone or expression. "One of the newly arrived families has a daughter who has caught his interest?"

All the elation from moments before deflated inside Eliza's chest. Apparently, she would have to come right out and say this. "No, that's not what I meant."

Augusta's relief was not the least bit hidden. "Thank the heavens." She shook her head, seeming to want to shake the idea away altogether. "If he's set his sights on another woman, I honestly don't know what I'll do. Truly, the more I think on my situation, the more convinced I am that Lord Lambert is my only hope."

"Come now," Eliza said, her stomach twisting. "There are any number of gentlemen who would be fawning all over you if you gave them a second look."

"Easy enough for you to say." Augusta's voice caught. "You who have another man waiting for you should nothing come of this Season."

"Excuse me?" Eliza had no notion what she meant and found

herself more than a little affronted that Augusta would imply such a thing.

"Mr. Collin," Augusta said. "A man does not visit a woman *every week* simply because they were once childhood friends. You should see the way he looks at you when you turn away. I am certain he only lacks a bit of courage, and once he finds it, he will offer for you posthaste."

Eliza took a small step back. She hadn't told her friend that Mr. Collin had offered for her *already*.

"Frankly, I have always wondered why you keep such a man around," Augusta continued, her tone turning bitter. "But now, I see the wisdom in it. If only you'd instructed me to keep such a man on hand in case the worst should happen, perhaps I would not be limited to only one option."

Eliza's head took to spinning. Between Augusta declaring she'd set her cap at Lord Lambert, indeed had declared him her only chance at happiness, and the way she'd spoken of Mr. Collin . . . she couldn't seem to think straight. Truly, she was suddenly struggling to *stand* straight.

"I never *kept him around*, as you called it, for any such purpose." Eliza never would have treated another human in such a manner. Still, she couldn't deny that she had never sent him off. She'd never asked him to keep visiting, but she certainly had never dissuaded him. Had she, unknowingly, urged Mr. Collin on?

Augusta dropped her hands to either side. "Regardless, you are safe. You have options and time. I have neither. The only chance I have is Lord Lambert. Please, say you understand and that you'll help me secure him."

Unfortunately, Eliza did understand.

She understood like few other women did what it felt like to live on the hem of society, supposedly a part of it but never truly accepted. Once the truth of Augusta's sister was known, and certainly, if she wasn't married by then, that was what she had to look forward to. A marriage, especially to a highly respected viscount, would stave off the worst, if not nearly all, of the ostracism.

Eliza looked at her friend. Truly looked. At her curls, forever perfectly curled. At her cheeks, blemish-free and smooth. At her gown, tailor-made just for this evening.

Augusta had a sweet heart and a generous nature. But she'd never had to work. She'd never had to see to it that her family got dinner at night because her single surviving parent was working late. She'd never had to walk down a street alone and hold her chin high despite the crass calls that followed her.

Augusta belonged here, between the chalked floors and draped ceilings, beside the well-cushioned chairs and readily available punch, among the polished gentlemen and elegant ladies. Even if she managed to keep one foot in society, her life would never again be the same if she didn't marry soon. Such a life—pushed aside by all, forced to be creative to keep meat on the table, alone for most of the time—it would crush Augusta.

Could Eliza do that to her friend?

No.

No matter the cost, she couldn't.

"Of course I'll help you," Eliza said, infusing as much confidence and encouragement as she could manage into those few words. Knowing what she was agreeing to, it hadn't amounted to much.

It was enough, though. For Augusta threw her arms about Eliza, hugging her tightly. "Thank you. Never have I needed a friend more than now, and I knew you would help me."

As she hugged Augusta back, Eliza couldn't even find it in herself to be pleased to be helping a friend. She only felt empty.

CHAPTER TWENTY

A dam lifted a bit of bread to his mouth but didn't take his eyes off Eliza where she sat atop a blanket only a few strides away. What the blazes had happened?

Two nights ago, he'd apologized—gads, he'd nearly kissed her—and he'd thought all was well between them again. He'd thought he was well on his way to securing her good opinion.

But ever since that night, Eliza had begun acting quite differently toward him. She'd begun avoiding him—he hadn't seen her again that night at Almack's, let alone been able to dance with her. Strangely enough, he'd seen Lady Augusta. He'd even gone so far as to dance with her twice, as she'd seemed to need the cheering. But he hadn't seen Eliza.

Then her father had written, declining his invitation to a family dinner last night. Was it Sir Mulgrave who actually disapproved of him and Eliza?

That didn't seem to make sense either. He'd spent many an afternoon at White's with Sir Mulgrave. They'd always been quite affable to one another. If not her father, then what?

Eliza, for her part, wasn't looking at him. Indeed, she'd chosen to sit with her back firmly toward him.

If it had been any other woman, he would have assumed she'd sat there for no true reason. Perhaps she was better shaded from the sun when facing that direction, or it was easier to converse with those who also sat on the blanket.

But not Eliza.

Not with all the time they'd shared or the words they'd spoken.

No, her back was toward him most decidedly on purpose.

If only he understood why.

"Lovely day for a picnic, isn't it?" Lady Augusta said, coming to sit beside him.

"Yes, quite," he agreed, standing and helping her down onto the blanket. "We are quite fortunate the weather has turned so fine."

"And that Lord and Lady Oakley thought to host a picnic and invite us."

"That as well." He sat back down, picking up his plate still full of food.

"Springtime has always been one of my favorite times of the year," Lady Augusta continued, not bothering with any of the food on her own plate. "The birds in the trees, the flowers all about. It always puts me in mind of weddings and love. Does it not for you as well, my lord?"

Adam paused with a bit of jam and biscuit halfway up to his mouth. What a strange question. "I can't say that it does," he answered, placing the food back down. Normally it put him in mind of a good bruising ride on Black Beard. The thought of his horse made his gaze turn toward Eliza. Had she gotten out as of late and ridden Starfire? He knew how much she loved riding.

"Yes, well, I suppose as a gentleman, such things are less important to you." Lady Augusta laughed—the light, twittering kind of giggle Adam had heard from any number of conniving ladies, but never from his friend.

"Tell me." Lady Augusta put her plate down—it seemed neither of them had much of an appetite just now. "How is our dear Miss Kitty? I have not seen her for several weeks now, and I long for her company."

Our Miss Kitty? "Lady Augusta, we are friends, are we not?"

"Certainly." She batted her lashes. "And perhaps . . . more?"

She was making no sense. "If we are friends, then perhaps you could be so kind as to explain to me what has happened."

She had the gall to actually look innocent and unknowing. "Whatever do you mean?"

Adam lifted a brow. "Eliza is *over there*, and not sitting with either you or me. You, on the other hand, have turned into some kind of . . ."

And then, all the pieces fell into place.

"Ah, blast." Adam dropped his head into an upturned hand. "You've set your cap at me." Which would explain both the change in her and why Eliza was suddenly ignoring him.

But why couldn't it be Eliza who was beside him steering the conversation toward marriage? He *knew* she understood he cared deeply for her. Though they'd never discussed anything permanent, was she so willing to walk away from him as all this? Did not her regard for him go any further than passing interest?

Augusta whispered low. "I don't see my preferring you to any other man is all that surprising." She sounded hurt; Adam most certainly could not like that. "We have spent quite a bit of time together this Season."

Yes, but looking back, Adam now understood he was drawn repeatedly toward the two women because of Eliza.

He sat up straight. "You have become a good friend." What else could a man say in such a situation as this? *I think you're lovely, but I currently have my eye on your best friend.* He didn't see that as going over well.

"But?" she pressed him.

"But, I need to speak with Miss Mulgrave for a moment." Standing quickly, he hurried over to Eliza's blanket. He didn't dare look back to see if Lady Augusta was watching him, puzzled, or if she was shooting daggers his direction with her eyes.

"Miss Mulgrave," he said, interrupting one of the two matrons who shared the blanket with Eliza. He neither knew nor cared to know their names. Right now, he only needed to see Eliza privately for a bit. "Would you care to take a turn about the garden with me?"

She didn't reply right away. But when no one else spoke, and he didn't leave, she finally said, "I have already seen it."

Why was she denying him such a small thing? "Please?" he asked.

"Very well." She stood without taking his offered hand and turned toward the gardens without so much as meeting his gaze.

They walked, side by side but not touching and not speaking, toward the well-tended flowers and hedges.

Eliza seemed unwilling to start, so that, it seemed, would fall to Adam. They turned down one of the small pebbled paths, and, content they were well out of earshot, Adam began.

"You, my dear, are avoiding me." When all else failed, bluntness often was the best approach.

"And if I am?"

"Then you are not denying it?" He'd thought, at the very least, she'd do that.

"Why should I? We both know I am."

He loved that she preferred bluntness, as he did. Blast, this would be much easier if he didn't keep finding new things to love about her.

"I should very much like to know why," he said.

Eliza stopped and turned toward him. Though her body faced him, she still didn't meet his eyes. "We are not so very suited to one another."

"Rubbish. We both love horses, taking the time to enjoy a quiet stroll, the minuet." Especially when he got to dance it with her. "We never disagree."

The corner of her lips ticked upward. "That's not entirely true."

"All right. Sometimes we disagree. But we always settle our disputes well enough in the end." He took hold of her hand and was pleased when she didn't pull away. "We are all the more dear to one another for it, are we not?"

"Adam"—his heart sped up at the sound of his name on her lips —"there's something you need to know."

That quelled most of the excitement. Whatever she was about to say next, he had a feeling it would change everything and not in the way he was hoping for.

"I was told this in the strictest of confidences, so you must swear to me that you will never repeat it to anyone. You will never tell that I told you."

"I swear it."

"Augusta's sister, Jane, has put Augusta in a rather delicate situation."

Lady Augusta's sister? "Don't tell me someone so wholly removed from either of us is the cause of this problem."

"She's not so removed as all that. Is not Augusta also our dear friend?"

"Yes." But not at all in the way Eliza was dear to him.

"Well, because of some decisions on her part, Jane has left Augusta with no other option than to wed soon."

Oh. *That* kind of a decision. There were only a few things a woman could do that would leave a younger sister in need of securing her future posthaste, and none of them were good.

"You need not tell me more," Adam said, stroking the back of Eliza's hand with his thumb. "So she has set her sights on me, then?"

"Yes."

"May I ask you something?"

Eliza's gaze jumped up, meeting his momentarily before dropping back down. "Certainly."

He moved up closer, pulling her nearer him. "Why did you not tell her that I'd already set my sights on *you?*"

"We had not . . . that is to say there wasn't . . ." Her voice grew smaller and smaller with each attempt to speak. "Nothing was settled."

Was, as in, now there wasn't the option available to them? "Then let's settle it."

"Adam, I can't."

"Why not? I care for Lady Augusta as well, but that doesn't mean *we* have to ignore all you and I have together." Did the *tendril* he felt for her not matter at all? The notion made his chest heat with frustration. "And what of yourself? Are you not worried for your own future?"

"I have options."

"Options?" What options? And she'd said the word without any passion or interest, even. Surely nothing that elicited such a platonic word to fall from her lips was worth pursuing.

"A childhood friend of mine, Mr. Collin. He's come to call on me every week for two months now."

Still no excitement, no spirit could he find in her tone or demeanor.

"Can you honestly tell me," Adam asked, dropping his head down, hoping to catch sight of her eyes. Maybe then he'd be able to read if she felt anything for him. "That you feel for him even half of what I feel for you?"

Her bottom lashes were lined with tears but none fell. "I can't," she whispered.

It wasn't much to hope on, but it was something. "Tell me you feel nothing for me, and I'll leave you be."

She closed her eyes, pressing two tears out. "I can't," she said again.

"Then why not tell Lady Augusta? We'll work together, you and I, and we'll find her someone. We'll see to it Society doesn't reject her wholly. We'll do something. Only please don't do *this.*"

"If I turn my back on Augusta now," Eliza said, "I'll never forgive myself. Augusta needs me to do this for her. She's been kind to me when no one else has been. She's shown herself to be generous, kindhearted, sincere. How can I abandon her now?"

"So instead, you will abandon us?"

"Please don't ask me not to."

Adam dropped her hand, pacing away. Was she really willing to put self-sacrifice before what they shared? He walked back toward her, unable to leave it there.

"You stood up to Lady Oakley when she spoke ill of Miss Notley. Why not do the same again? Why not speak up, if not for me then at least for yourself?"

For the first time, Eliza's voice turned firm, very nearly hard. "I have been *told* to be many things since coming to London. I have been pushed to be more flirty. I have been pushed to be more silent. I have *tried* to be any number of things—the woman who laughs lightly, the young lady who dances elegantly. I guess, whatever I am or am not, it's not enough. Not for you or anyone."

"Eliza, I didn't mean——"

"Have you not heard them today?" She placed a hand against her forehead, her eyes conveying the depth of her pain. "Even still, they whisper of my uncouth comments, my inability to act as refined and elegant as they all expect. I can barely be among Society for more than a quarter of an hour before the stares and whispers start. Is this what the rest of my life would be like if we . . .?"

"No," he said firmly. "We could make it work. Society will accept you in time; I swear to you they will."

Her voice dropped low. "Oh, Adam, I grow so tired of the constant rejection."

"It won't last forever."

Her eyes met his. "But it will for Augusta if we don't do this for her. And she wouldn't be able to handle it, Adam. She isn't used to a hard life or being unwanted among society. It would crush her, and I think you know that."

For the first time, Adam felt himself wavering. What she said was true. If Lady Augusta could not secure a husband for herself, there would be consequences, and harsh ones, at that. No matter his love for Eliza, Lady Augusta was still a good friend, one he did not want to see hurting for the actions of her sister.

Eliza lifted her skirt and backed up. "So you see, this is for the best. The best for everyone."

Adam ached to say something. But what? What argument was there that she had not already countered? What argument did he still have?

"Eliza," he whispered, "I love you."

She briefly closed her eyes, her hands still clenching her skirts. "Yes, and I am sorry for it."

That was all she had to say? He searched her face. Did she not care for him at all? Her expression was firm, unwavering. She truly was saying goodbye. Unequivocally so.

"I guess the truth of the matter is," Eliza said, taking another step away from him, "I'm not that audacious after all." Turning, she hurried off.

CHAPTER TWENTY-ONE

A week had passed since last Adam had seen Eliza. A full week of calling on her, of hoping to steal a moment with her while at the same gathering, of wracking his brain to find a way to simply talk with her.

Her goodbye had been unquestionable and unchangeable—yet he questioned it, and he desperately wanted to change it. If only she'd give him a chance.

All his efforts were to no avail. Eliza, it seemed, had shut herself up in her bedchamber and refused to come out if there was any chance he would be present. He'd even gone so far as to corner Sir Mulgrave at White's and not-so-subtly hint that the two of them should go horseback riding together—and of course that Sir Mulgrave ought to invite Eliza, since she enjoyed it so much.

In the end, he had gone horseback riding alone.

Now, he sat across from Lady Augusta as his carriage driver turned them about Hyde Park. Yet another failed attempt to draw Eliza out. Perhaps it had best be his last.

If Eliza did not wish to see him, he should respect that desire.

It was a knife to his heart, but he wouldn't press himself upon Eliza, no matter his love for her. After all, if a man truly loved a woman, did he not listen to her and allow her to make up her own mind on such matters? He would not taint his love for her by disregarding her wishes any longer.

Lady Augusta talked on and on. As much as he'd failed to see Eliza this week, he'd never seen so much of Lady Augusta. She was never embarrassingly clinging, yet everywhere he went, there she was, too. She and her father had sat with him during the musicale last Tuesday; she'd persuaded him to dance with her twice at a ball; she had been present every time he'd tried to catch Eliza during her family's at-home. If he hadn't known what was happening, her actions would have puzzled him greatly.

But Eliza was right. Even desperate for a match, as he knew she was, Lady Augusta was still all grace and generosity and kindness. Her actions were a bit forward, but still, she did nothing that would evoke censure. Adam watched her as Lady Augusta turned her face toward the tall tree they were passing under. A man could certainly do worse.

Still, she wasn't Eliza. She wasn't the woman who made his heart race or invigorated his mind. She wasn't the one he fell asleep thinking about or the first thought he had when he awoke.

He'd hoped to speak with Eliza once more before telling Lady Augusta what he knew. However, he could see the strain of the weight she bore etching deeper and deeper lines about her mouth. He could see from the now constant droop of her shoulders that Lady Augusta was nearing her breaking point. Though she wasn't the woman he loved, he did care about her as a friend. It seemed the time to stay silent had come to an end.

"Lady Augusta," he began.

"Yes, my lord?" She spoke prettily, though not quite as she had when they were friends and both content to be nothing more.

"I have a confession."

Her smile slipped a bit.

Adam opened his mouth, ready to tell her exactly what Eliza had told him. Only, he hesitated. If he admitted to Lady Augusta what Eliza had said, might she not be angry at Eliza? Might it not

THE AUDACIOUS MISS ELIZA

make Lady Augusta mortified? He couldn't do that to either woman.

"I have to admit"—he had to think of another way to broach this topic, something more delicate and something fast—"I have not been ignorant to the sudden change . . . between us." If he gave her an opening, would she take it?

"Oh?" She even went so far as to bat her lashes. "I thought it was common, as a gentleman and lady grew to know one another better, for their relationship to change, to become something more permanent."

This was by far the boldest he'd ever seen her. Instead of endearing her to him, however, it only angered Adam. "Eliza told me."

Lady Augusta's face instantly paled. "Told you? Whatever do you mean?"

"About your sister."

There was silence between them for quite some time.

Lady Augusta seemed to be jumping between furious and terrified.

Adam shook his head. He hadn't wanted her upset, he'd only wanted her to be honest.

"Listen. What your sister did, that was her choice. It doesn't change how I see you."

"Then you are a rarity among society." Her voice was weak.

How he sincerely hoped she wasn't about to faint. "I understand *why* you are acting this way. I just wanted you to know that. And to know that you could have just told me outright, yourself."

"A lady could hardly have such a conversation with a gentleman."

Eliza had shared such a conversation with him. He desperately missed the open honesty that he always found with her. Why couldn't she just speak with him, even once more?

"And now that you know?" Lady Augusta asked.

He wished he could say that he wasn't her only option. But he didn't feel that would be completely true. The news of her sister would reach Town sooner or later, and it would significantly damage her chances of making a good match. He wasn't going to lie and tell her otherwise.

"If we did . . . make a match of it." Gads, but those words were hard to get out. "Is there anyone who might be . . . unhappy?"

Lady Augusta looked sincerely surprised. "Who would be unhappy? My parents adore you—I know they do. I love Miss Kitty; you would never need worry I would be unkind toward her. I suppose I don't know your cousins particularly well, but I'm sure we could be good friends given some time."

He'd hoped to lead her to the conclusion that perhaps Eliza would be hurt by their connection. "Any of our friends, perhaps?"

Again, she only looked surprised. "I think they all would be quite pleased with the match." She listed her head. "Tell me, my lord, is there someone *you* think would be unhappy?"

"What of Miss Mulgrave?"

Lady Augusta smiled, her eyes shining. "Is that what has you worried?"

It was, quite a lot so.

"Silly man," she said, far too cheerfully for his liking. "She would be delighted. Her two dearest friends, finding happiness together? I am sure she will be beside herself."

Is that what Lady Augusta thought? Adam suddenly felt quite sick to his stomach. Eliza's decision to choose Augusta's future happiness over her own went so far as to not even admit her own feelings to her closest friend. He both admired her for it and heartily wished she was just a little less selfless. Perhaps then she wouldn't have rejected him.

Lady Augusta reached out and placed her gloved hand over his own. "You are too kind, Lord Lambert, to think that Eliza might be made to feel uncomfortable at our connection. That truly is most thoughtful of you."

Thoughtful was not the right word, but if Eliza hadn't enlightened Augusta before now, he saw no reason to be the one to do it. Between Eliza's words from a week ago, the realization she hadn't even bothered to correct her friend, and days and days of her shutting him out, Adam knew she had made up her mind. All he could do was go against her wishes or respect them. And only a cad disrespected a lady's wishes.

"You see," Lady Augusta said, her voice soft once more, "by all accounts, we would make an excellent match."

Adam eyed the woman next to him; she *was* a dear friend, even if friendship was all he felt for her. Every day he made Lady Augusta wait for a proposal put her at that much more risk of being ostracized from society. Though Lady Augusta was not the woman of his dreams—*that* woman had shut him out completely—she was kindhearted and he did not doubt that they would be happy enough together. More still, Lady Augusta was out of time. They all were.

"You are a very good woman, Lady Augusta."

To his surprise, tears formed at the corner of her eyes. "Please." Her voice caught. "Will you save me?"

It's what Eliza wanted—for him to save Lady Augusta. It was the only thing she'd ever asked of him.

"Very well," he said. "Lady Augusta, would you do me the honor of becoming my wife?"

CHAPTER TWENTY-TWO

E liza stared out her bedchamber window, looking down at the road as Lord Down took his leave. Somewhere, in the back of her mind, she knew she ought to speak with Dinah about the way she was encouraging the man's attentions. How any woman could stand Lord Down, Eliza would never understand.

But, right now, she couldn't seem to make herself care. Eliza leaned back, away from the window, allowing the curtain to block her view. She couldn't seem to care about anything.

I love you.

Adam's words from a week before echoed about her mind. No matter what she did, no matter how much time she put between herself and that fateful moment, the memory never seemed to fade.

And it never seemed to hurt any less.

Augusta had been by yesterday. Without asking for permission first, Dinah had shown Augusta into Eliza's room and left the two of them together. Her family had probably been hoping the meeting would cheer her up.

Eliza let out a derisive chuckle. Her family had never been more wrong.

She stood and crossed to her bed. Taking hold of the blanket, she fluffed it for what must have been the dozenth time today. Instead of taking her mind off how desperately she missed Adam, Augusta had admitted that she was engaged to him. Eliza's hands stilled, the blanket slowly falling back to the bed. Adam had finally given in. She had always guessed that if she kept away from him long enough, he'd realize Augusta was running out of time, and he'd do the right thing. Augusta had said that they were keeping the engagement quiet until they announced it in front of all their friends at a large dinner party Adam was throwing.

That party would be tonight.

While Eliza knew it was the right thing to do—truthfully, the only thing to be done—she couldn't help but be heartbroken all the same.

There was a soft knock at the door and Lady Blackmore peeked in. "Mr. Collin has come, Eliza. He's asking to speak with you in particular."

"Thank you, Lady Blackmore, but please tell him I have a headache." Eliza repeated the lie she'd been using for just over a week now.

Instead of leaving once again, as Eliza expected of her, Lady Blackmore stepped into her room and shut the door behind her.

"We need to talk." The woman made her way to the small settee near the hearth and sat herself down, patting the seat beside her.

Eliza should have known she wouldn't escape such a thing forever. But, she seemed unable to care that it was happening now. She moved over to the settee and sat.

"You still refuse to call me Charlotte," Lady Blackmore began. "Even though I know I've said you could any number of times."

She hadn't expected this line of conversation.

"Do you know why I think that is?" Lady Blackmore continued. Eliza shook her head.

"I think it's because you haven't yet decided if you belong here or not. You haven't decided if you want to stay here, with the elegant houses, the titles, the social niceties. I don't think you know yet if this is what you want for your future."

Eliza's brow creased. "I'd never thought of it that way."

Lady Blackmore turned atop the settee, facing her more fully. "Your father's knighthood happened to you. It wasn't your choice. And, perhaps because of that, or possibly because of any number of things, you haven't decided for yourself if this is really where you want to be. I'm guessing that's why you haven't told Mr. Collin farewell. That's also why you haven't made your feelings for Lord Lambert clear."

Eliza's face burned. Heavens, how could she ever hope to be accepted by society if she could *never* control her emotions?

Lady Blackmore laughed softly. "Do not worry. It was clear to me you have been quite in love with him for some time now, yet you have always acted with decorum and poise. I could not be more proud."

Eliza's lips ticked upward. "That's probably because I didn't realize how in love I was with him until only a week ago. If I'd known as much myself, I'd have probably been the worst type of fool."

Lady Blackmore laughed. "Love is a painful bliss, is it not?"

Eliza nodded. For her, it had been far more painful and far less bliss. But she understood all the same.

"May I ask," Lady Blackmore said, "if you know now, why all the headaches? Has he rejected you?"

"I rejected him."

"What?"

Amid tears and a few hiccups, Eliza relayed the whole of the story. She prayed Augusta would forgive her for telling her secret to yet another person, but Eliza simply could not hold all the loneliness and ache inside anymore, and Lady Blackmore had proven herself the best of confidences.

"Oh, my darling girl," Lady Blackmore said when she was finally finished with all. "Why did you not say something to Augusta at the first?"

"I had only realized myself the extent of my feelings for Adam." It was blessedly beautiful to say his name aloud, and thankfully Lady Blackmore did not criticize her for it. "I wasn't ready to speak them aloud. More still, Augusta was right. If I didn't marry Adam, I would be fine. But if she didn't, it would mean her end."

"Socially."

"Pardon?"

"You would be fine, *socially*. And Augusta would suffer, *socially*. But Eliza, sweetheart, surely you have not begun to think that what society believes is of the utmost importance? What of your heart? What of Augusta's? And, dare I say it, what of Lord Lambert's?"

"Oh, I don't know——"

"I think you do." Lady Blackmore placed a hand gently against Eliza's cheek. "I think you do know exactly where his heart lies." She leaned forward, whispering, "I think we both know it lies with you."

"But what of Augusta?"

"A marriage to a viscount would be a boon to your friend, all the more so when news of her sister's actions are made known. I won't deny that it's true. However, just because that is so doesn't mean you should stay silent now. You've spoken up to acquaintances and neighbors before. This time, you need to speak up to a friend."

"What if she hates me for it?"

"I don't know her well enough to promise you she won't. But that doesn't change things. This is still something you need to do, regardless of who it is you're standing up to."

Eliza nodded. "No matter who is present, I still have to be myself." Adam had asked as much from her. It was the woman she'd always wanted to be.

"Or," Lady Blackmore said, "you can go downstairs and accept Mr. Collin. Your life will be comfortable enough and similar to the one you enjoyed growing up. Moreover, such a station in life will put you in the path of other women whose lives have played out closer to yours. There is a good chance you won't ever have to stand up to anyone again. But is that really what you want?"

Tears blurred Eliza's vision. "I want to be as courageous as Father."

"You've always been that, dear." Lady Blackmore stood. "I wouldn't wait, though, if I were you. The time to be courageous is often short, and once it has passed, it never comes again. And don't worry about Augusta. She has a loving family and friends in high places." She gestured to herself with a bit of a laugh.

Lady Blackmore—Charlotte—moved over to the door and pulled it open. "What message should I give Mr. Collin?"

Eliza blinked several times and the room came back into view. "Tell him I will be down shortly." Standing, she faced Charlotte. "I believe it's time I tell him goodbye."

CHAPTER TWENTY-THREE

E liza reached the Honeyfields' house just as they were all climbing into a carriage. Eliza stepped out of hers and hurried over, catching hold of Augusta by the arm.

"We need to talk."

Lady Honeyfield spoke before Augusta could. "Miss Mulgrave, what a pleasant surprise. We have missed you this week. I do hope you are feeling better."

"Thank you, my lady, I am." She *was* feeling better—better enough to truly speak her mind. Eliza turned back toward Augusta. "Might we have a minute?"

"You are free to ride with us," Lord Honeyfield said, ushering them all toward the waiting carriage. "You young ladies can gossip on the way."

Augusta squeezed Eliza's arm. "I'm so glad you are well enough to join us tonight."

"No, Augusta," Eliza said. "We need to talk first."

Her brow creased and a wariness entered her eyes. "Don't tell me word of Jane has already arrived?"

"It has nothing to do with your sister," Eliza assured her.

"Thank goodness for that," Lady Honeyfield said, her gaze

turning toward Eliza and hardening. "Now if you don't mind, tonight is very important for Augusta, and we must be on our way." She took Augusta's arm and began pulling her daughter toward the carriage.

"Let her ride with me," Eliza said, motioning toward the conveyance she rode up in. "Our driver is quite trustworthy, and we will be there in no time at all."

"Why not you two ride with us?" Lady Honeyfield asked.

Why not . . . Eliza very well couldn't explain the *actual* reason. "It is only a little on-dit that I heard, and we shall be quite too tight all four of us in your carriage to truly enjoy the diversion."

Lady Honeyfield looked confused.

And well she should. Eliza was never going to be known for her lithe tales. It was a pity Dinah wasn't here.

"But," Lord Honeyfield said, "two young women cannot arrive at Lord Lambert's house alone."

"Did not I tell you?" Eliza continued, summoning every ounce of practice and advice on keeping her blush hidden. "My father is riding with us. You did not suppose I came alone, did you?"

Lord Honeyfield instantly smiled. "Of course not. You two young ladies go have your gossip. We will see you at Lambert's."

Eliza took hold of Augusta's arm and pulled her toward her own carriage before Lady Honeyfield could object. The footman was quick—he had learned to be after being employed by Sir Mulgrave—and got their door open just as they reached the conveyance. Eliza all but pushed her friend inside as she instructed the driver to follow the Honeyfield's carriage.

"But . . ." Augusta looked about the empty carriage. "You said Sir Mulgrave had accompanied you."

"Yes." Eliza sat across from her as the footman closed the door behind her. "And if it hadn't been for all your excellent advice on the matter, I never would have been able to control my blush enough to get away with it."

Augusta tittered a nervous laugh. "I don't know if I should be delighted or disturbed that I trained you so well."

"Whichever you feel like being, do so quickly, for I have much to say and none of it, I fear, will be well-received."

"Such foreboding." Augusta laughed again. It was a little less uneasy than before, but only barely. "I am all anticipation."

"Augusta," Eliza said, meeting her friend's gaze. "I have to tell you something."

"I was getting that impression, yes."

Eliza fought the smile. "Stop making light, or I shall never get through this."

Augusta pressed her mouth together so tightly, her lips nearly disappeared.

"You know," Eliza tried once more, "that as your friend, I only want the best for you. Your happiness is so very important."

Augusta nodded but blessedly didn't interrupt.

"That being said . . ." This was the tricky part. "I have come to learn, partially through your kindness and partially through just living here in London among all the titled gentlemen and ladies, that my happiness matters as well."

"But of course it does," Augusta blurted, leaning forward.

Eliza held up a hand.

Augusta bolted back upright and snapped her mouth shut. She gave Eliza a firm nod to continue.

"Oh, botheration," Eliza said with a little laugh. "You know this would be so much easier if you weren't so nice."

"What would be?"

"I'm trying to tell you something important."

"Something important, yes, I know." Augusta nodded, urging her to continue. "Something that will make you happy."

"I'm in love with Lord Lambert."

The moment the words rushed from Eliza the mood in the carriage shifted. It turned cold, and Augusta stilled. Truly she looked almost frozen. One hand up, mid-wave, her mouth partially open.

"I'm sorry," Eliza said. "I ought to have told you before now."

Slowly, Augusta's suspended hand dropped into her lap. "I know." She sighed and leaned back against the squabs once more.

"You knew?"

Augusta's mouth pulled to one side even as her opposing eyebrow lifted. "All those times you laughed with one another, danced together, talked horses together, I was there, too. How could I not know? I have seen you two slowly falling for one another for weeks now."

"Why didn't you say anything?" And here Eliza thought the surprise would all be on her friend's part.

"At first, I was worried it would scare you away. I saw the way you shrunk when around Society. The way you hid yourself, in part, whenever someone of position addressed you. I was never sure what it was about Lord Lambert that put you at ease, but I wasn't about to mess it all up by opening my big mouth."

"And when news came of your sister?"

Augusta's gaze dropped to their slippers. "I was too cowardly then. He hadn't spoken for you, and you hadn't said anything about him, and I convinced myself it was all my imagination." She blinked a few times, her gaze flitting toward the door. "I was *desperate.*"

"So," Eliza said at length, "what do we do now?"

Augusta still wouldn't meet her gaze. "I don't know."

They were silent for a few minutes and then the carriage rolled to a stop. There was the usual clatter of the footman dismounting. Then the door swung open.

"One more minute, if you please," Augusta said, sounding quite as though her world hadn't been wholly upended in the few minutes they'd been riding.

"Yes, my lady," the footman said with a bow and then closed the door.

"He loves you, too, you know," Augusta said.

Eliza's heart gave a lurch, his words from the picnic echoing about her head yet again. She'd thought back on that moment so many times, she'd almost begun to wonder if she'd imagined it.

Augusta switched sides to sit beside Eliza. "I was a coward before, and I pray you can forgive me. But right now, it is time we do something about this mess of ours."

"I was afraid that standing up for myself would mean hurting a friend." It was still something that niggled at the back of Eliza's mind.

"No, your bravery in coming to see me was not only awe-inspiring, it was also very considerate. And so, I think I shall have the courage after all to end my engagement with Lord Lambert."

"Truly?"

Augusta rocked her head back and forth. "Well, 'ending' maybe isn't the right word since, according to society, we aren't even engaged yet. Perhaps, 'prevent' would be a better word."

Eliza threw her arms around Augusta. "You are the dearest friend."

"Me? You are the one who was willing to give up your own love to save a friend."

Eliza pulled back. "Are you certain you will be all right?"

Augusta gave her a bittersweet smile. "My mother and father will fret something awful, but only because they love me. Then we shall probably all return to the country for the rest of the season. By next year the rumors and gossip will have settled, and I'll return for a second *first* Season." She ended with a flourish of her gloved hand.

Eliza laughed. "I guess all that remains now is to let Adam know of the change."

"Oh my, yes." Augusta's eyes turned wide. "We'd hate for him to announce an engagement to me *now*."

"We'll have to speak with him before he does so."

"Augusta, dear?" Lord Honeyfield called from outside. "Are you coming?"

Augusta opened the door a crack. "Just a minute, Father. We'll be right out."

"We shouldn't keep Lord Lambert waiting," her mother called.

"He won't mind," Augusta said. "Especially not after I tell him the on-dit Eliza just shared with me. But I can hardly do that if I don't get the whole of it first." She shut the door and wheeled back around toward Eliza. "I don't even know when he plans to make the announcement. Besides, it shouldn't be *we* who talk to him. It needs to be *you*, alone."

Eliza shook her head, noticing the footman still waiting patiently just outside the carriage door. "He wouldn't dare a private tête-à-tête with another woman moments before he plans to announce an engagement."

"Not even for you?" Augusta's brow dropped low. "No, probably not." She sighed. "Face it, Eliza. You picked far too honorable a gentleman. Next time, you should set your sights a bit lower."

Eliza laughed, swatting at her friend's shoulder. "Come, now. How about this. You go in and give him the message to come out here. I'll wait in the carriage. No one will be the wiser that he's actually come out to speak with a woman at all."

Augusta giggled, but it was a bit high and far too forced. "Me? Send a gentleman out to speak, secretly, with a lady? I don't know if I dare."

"We all have to be bold sometimes. Audacious, even."

"Audacious?" Augusta shuttered. "I don't think I was ever cut out to be so."

"Then do it for a friend." If Augusta didn't go through with this, there was a very real chance Adam *would* announce the engagement before Eliza could talk to him. What a fool she'd been. He'd been dying to talk with her all week, and what had she done? Hid away. Now that she couldn't talk to him, she was desperate to.

"Very well." Augusta squared her shoulders. "For you, I'll do it." She faced the door. "Audacious. Be audacious," she said to herself. "The audacious Lady Augusta." She turned back toward Eliza, pulling a face. "That sounds terrible. The audacious Miss Eliza is much better. Perhaps you ought to give him the message yourself."

"Just go already." Eliza placed her hands against Augusta's back and gave her a gentle shove.

"All right, all right." Augusta opened the carriage door and hopped out. She hurried up the stairs, barely allowing her parents time to catch up before she reached the door.

"And you, miss?" the footman asked Eliza.

"I'll be waiting here for now. But *when* Lord Lambert comes out," she forced herself to say *when* instead of *if*, "will you direct him to this carriage?"

"Very well, miss."

Blessedly, he didn't ask questions. Instead, he shut the door softly.

Leaving Eliza in the carriage alone.

Waiting.

Hoping she'd get the opportunity to explain to Adam.

Praying she wasn't too late.

CHAPTER TWENTY-FOUR

Adam, with Aunt Priscilla beside him, welcomed guest after guest into his house. He'd told his aunt that he was making a big announcement tonight but nothing more than that. He'd meant to tell her of his intention to become engaged to Lady Augusta, but the words had died on his tongue every time he'd tried to utter them. So long as he could push through them tonight, he'd never have to say them again. The rumor mill would see to that.

It was a small consolation.

"Good evening," he said with a smile that felt plastered onto his face. "Thank you so much for coming." Did he sound as fake to others as he did to his own ears?

"Welcome, welcome," Aunt Priscilla said.

Lady Augusta hurried through the front door and very nearly collided with him.

"Good evening," he said, the only variation between what he'd said to the past dozen guests and to her was the uptick in his voice due to surprise.

"My lord," she said hastily. "We need to talk."

"Welcome, Lady Augusta," Aunt Priscilla cooed. "Lady Honeyfield, Lord Honeyfield, you are most welcome."

"Please," Lady Augusta whispered. "Might we just step out front for a bit?"

"Dear," Lady Honeyfield said, taking her daughter's elbow. "You will have plenty of time *later*." Her mother pulled her away and into the drawing room.

Adam kept an eye on her as she was unceremoniously nudged into the next room. Just before he lost sight of her, she turned toward him and pointed out toward the front door. "Go," she mouthed.

Then she was swallowed up in the crush that was slowly but effectively overtaking his home.

He shook his head. What the blazes had that been about? Adam turned and smiled, welcoming in yet another guest, but his mind didn't leave Lady Augusta. Had she wanted to talk with him? Or show him something outside? Either way, he very well couldn't leave at the moment.

Finally, all the guests were assembled. Adam entered the drawing room with Aunt Priscilla on his arm. Theodosia and Earnest had been permitted to join them tonight, and he quickly spotted them with a couple of guests closer to their own age all crowded around a chessboard. A couple of the young men kept throwing Theodosia glances, though she appeared too wrapped up in the chess game to notice. Adam was going to have to watch out for her when she finally made her bows to society.

Leaving Aunt Priscilla with Lady Oakley, he made his way over to where Lady Augusta stood with her parents.

"I am pleased to see you all here this evening," he said.

Lord Honeyfield gave the largest smile he'd ever seen on the man as Lady Honeyfield simpered, "As if we would miss tonight of all nights." Both parents then turned toward Lady Augusta, their smiles broadening still more. Adam hadn't thought it possible.

All that merriment, and he only felt the more sick for it.

As his own gaze turned toward Lady Augusta, however, where he expected to see happiness only bested by that of her parents, he saw a fake smile and hesitation in her gaze.

"I believe," he said to Lady Augusta, "you and I ought to take a turn about the room." Not that there was hardly any room to turn about in. Why *had* Aunt Priscilla thought it necessary to invite so many people?

"Thank you. That sounds wonderful." Lady Augusta rested her hand atop his arm, and they turned away from her parents. The moment they were two steps away, Lady Augusta leaned in, her words rapid and firm. "You need to go outside, out front. There's *someone* there—"

"Lord Lambert." Lady Oakley moved toward them. "Allow me to express my deep gratitude for being invited tonight. It is quite an honor. All the more so as I can see you have recently decided to *improve* the quality of the guests you allow into your home."

"Pardon me?" Adam was at quite a loss as to what she'd meant.

Lady Oakley waved a hand back and forth. "Far be it from me to put another down, only I'd noticed the absence of Miss Mulgrave."

Adam's jaw ground tight. "Then perhaps I may inform you that I did *indeed* invite the Mulgrave family. Only they sent their deepest regrets; a previous engagement kept them from attending."

"Oh?" Lady Oakley said. "Well, certainly no one would fault you for *not* inviting them."

"Although . . ." Lady Augusta suddenly spoke up. "If they *had* decided to come, last minute, they might be in a carriage out front. This very minute. Just waiting to be told the invitation still stands."

Lady Oakley's brow dropped low. "Waiting outside in a carriage? That would be very odd indeed."

Even more odd was the nervous way Lady Augusta was acting. Was she feeling as unready for the announcement as he? Perhaps they could postpone? Wait for another day to make anything known?

No, that was ridiculous. Everyone was gathered—and it seemed half the gathered party already suspected an announcement of some kind. He didn't know Augusta's feelings on their situation, but he knew full well a couple of days was not going to be enough to settle his stomach.

"If you will excuse us," Adam said, "there are a few other guests we hoped to speak with before dinner is announced."

Lady Oakley curtsied and moved off. She was probably ruffled to know that the Mulgraves had been invited, but Adam didn't care. He'd much rather have the kindness and sincerity the Mulgraves brought to his house over the superiority and pomp of someone like Lady Oakley.

"Really, you need to go out front," Lady Augusta tried again. "Like I was trying to tell you, Eliza—"

What about her?

"Adam." Aunt Priscilla came over. "I think it's time."

"Just a minute." He turned back toward Lady Augusta. "What of Eliza?"

"She's not here," Aunt Priscilla said, not backing down. "Whatever your announcement is, I think we'd all like to hear it." She spoke loud enough that the half of the room closest to them turned their way. At the sudden stillness, the other half grew instantly curious and turned their way as well.

Why couldn't everyone just leave them alone for a minute? But apparently, that was not to be. The entire room watched him, waiting, expecting him to speak.

"Miss Kitty," Lady Augusta said suddenly. "I haven't seen her yet today and I know she is just dying to show me her new ribbons." Without another word, Lady Augusta pulled away from him and hurried out of the room.

Adam stared after her. He very well couldn't make the announcement now. Not without her by his side. He turned back to find the room still waiting.

He opened his mouth. "Dinner will be served in a few minutes . . . if you could all be patient just a little longer."

That seemed to satisfy most of them, and they turned back to their own conversations.

"What was the meaning of that?" Aunt Priscilla asked. "Why not tell them the announcement?"

"I think you are more eager to learn of it than anyone," Adam said, hoping to throw her off the scent.

Unfortunately, Aunt Priscilla was too much of a bloodhound. "Is there a reason you cannot announce right now?"

"Not without Lady Augusta, I can't."

Relief instantly flooded her features. "I was hoping it would be her." Aunt Priscilla patted his cheeks. "This home needs a woman's touch."

Adam shook his head, pulling away from her. He, for one, hadn't hoped it would be Lady Augusta.

"Pardon me, my lord," Mr. Reid said, coming over to him.

Adam turned eagerly toward his butler. "Yes?" Anything to get away from his aunt just now.

"There is a carriage out front, but the driver refuses to take himself off."

Adam glanced about the room. Was there still a guest not yet in attendance? He'd thought everyone was here. He turned back toward Aunt Priscilla. "Are we missing anyone?"

She, too, was searching the room. "I'm certain we are not. Do you recognize the carriage?" she asked Mr. Reid.

"No, my lady."

"Well," Adam wasn't sure what the problem was, but he couldn't very well go see to it himself, "please take care of it."

"Yes, my lord." With a bow, Mr. Reid walked off.

"Now you stay here," Aunt Priscilla said, "and I'll go bring Lady Augusta down. Just as soon as you two are standing side by side, you can make the announcement."

Lord and Lady Honeyfield moved up closer to him, apparently having heard his aunt, and nodded their approval vigorously.

"Very well," Adam said.

His aunt was gone in the blink of an eye. This was it. They would be engaged within mere minutes.

And they *would* be happy together. He was determined they would be. No matter what it took, or how long it took to forget Eliza, they would be——

A commotion brought his head round. There was female arguing coming from the corridor. What the blazes was it now?

Never had Adam attended—let alone held—a party where so many things seemed to go awry.

Adam excused himself from Lord and Lady Honeyfield and stepped back out into the corridor. The front door was open, and he could hear Mr. Reid arguing with the driver of the strange carriage out front. Aunt Priscilla stood at the base of the stairs, a determined-looking Miss Notley blocking her passage.

"I order you to step aside this minute," Aunt Priscilla said. "Or you shall be thrown out without a recommendation."

Miss Notley stood her ground. "I'm sorry, my lady, but I am to speak with his lordship *before* Lady Augusta is brought down."

"I don't care." Aunt Priscilla was nearly shouting.

"Begging your pardon," Miss Notley's voice was far more calm, "but neither do I. I shall stay here and do as necessary."

Adam shook his head. This night was getting stranger and stranger all the time. He placed a hand against his aunt's back. "Why don't you head back into the drawing room and entertain our guests? I'll deal with this."

Muttering under her breath, Aunt Priscilla lifted her skirts and fairly flew into the drawing room.

Adam turned toward Miss Notley and folded his arms. "You had better have a very good reason for what you did, or you will be turned out of this house."

Miss Notley only lifted her chin and then turned and called up the stairs. "It's all right now, my lady. It's only his lordship down here."

Lady Augusta appeared suddenly at the top of the stairs. She rushed down, even as Miss Notley began walking up. They met in the middle.

"Thank you," Lady Augusta said, pressing her own cheek against the cheek of the governess.

"Anything for Miss Mulgrave," Miss Notley said, then continued climbing the stairs.

"Miss Notley," Adam called after her, "We aren't through talking."

"Calm down," Lady Augusta said, reaching the bottom stair.

210

"Once you hear what she's done, you'll be more likely to up her wage then toss her out."

Adam opened his mouth to ask exactly what was going on, but Lady Augusta stopped him with a hand.

"Don't say anything. Just listen. Eliza come to see me this afternoon. I knew it before, but I was too much a coward to say anything. But we talked and she admitted to the whole thing and now I just can't see myself going through with it and so she wants to speak with you and though I think it's to accept your hand, I guess I'd be getting ahead of myself if I said it was——"

Adam took hold of her hand, silencing her. "Lady Augusta, what are you talking about?"

She scrunched her nose up. "I told Eliza I wasn't going to do this right." She took a breath and started again. "Eliza is out in the carriage. She wants to speak to you. She admitted to me that she loves you——"

Adam spun on his heel and hurried toward the door.

"——and I told her you felt the same," Lady Augusta called after him.

"Never mind, Mr. Reid," Adam called as he passed the butler. He flung the carriage door open. Sure enough, there sat Eliza, the bit of skirt fabric beneath her hands a well-wrinkled mess.

"Adam," she said, almost a whisper.

"Is it true?" he asked. "Do you love me?"

She looked at him, then a smile spread across her face and she nodded.

CHAPTER TWENTY-FIVE

T he smile on Eliza's face grew from small, to full, and on until it hurt, and Eliza was certain it would break her face. Adam climbed in beside her, allowing the door to slam shut behind him.

He didn't bother to sit but knelt before. "My dearest, please say you'll be mine. Please promise me we'll ride horses in the warm months and gossip about our neighbors during the cold ones."

"Why, Lord Lambert," Eliza said, for once not carrying one whit that her face was no doubt red as roses. "One might begin to suspect you care particularly for me if you continue on so."

"Didn't I tell you?" he asked. "I love you. I love you ardently, I love you completely." He took hold of her hands and pulled her close to him. "I love you wildly and madly."

"How perfect. I love you that way, too."

He lifted a hand and cupped her face. "We almost missed one another, didn't we?"

It scared Eliza to think how close they had come to losing one another. "Yes, we did."

"But I should have known all along someone as audacious as you would not have allowed that to happen."

Eliza shook her head. "I almost did."

"*Almost* isn't nearly as important as *did*." He shifted and sat beside her.

"You know . . ." Eliza scooted over to make space for him, but not too much. She wanted him near. "You are quite like Black Beard in many ways."

Adam looked off into the distance. "Breathtaking in my handsomeness?"

Eliza laughed. She was feeling positively giddy. "Yes. Handsome for sure. Breathtaking, in a way, with your title and place in society. But, deep down, really you're just a sweetheart."

"Is that a good thing?" He wrapped an arm around her, drawing her in.

"It's exactly the kind of man I wish to be with for the rest of my life."

"I like the sound of that—the rest of our lives."

Eliza rested her head against his shoulder. "Though I might have a few things to say about what you are wearing. Didn't anyone ever tell you that dark purple breeches should never be worn with that color of green jacket?"

Adam only nodded. "I wasn't exactly in the mood earlier today to look my best."

"Quite frankly, I've been meaning to tell you, *nothing* goes with this color of green jacket."

"Sure it does," Adam said, pulling away from her and slipping it off. He draped it around her shoulders, tugging on the lapels and bringing their faces together. "You do." He leaned in and placed a soft kiss on her lips. "In fact, I've been meaning to tell *you* that everything in my wardrobe looks better when you're with me."

"I love you, Adam," she whispered.

"I love you, too, Eliza."

He kissed her again, more fervently this time.

And when the guests came knocking at the carriage door, they just kept right on kissing.

EPILOGUE

Lady Charlotte Blackmore looked out over the veritable sea of people. The engagement party for Eliza and Lord Lambert was going to be talked about for months to come—possibly years. Of course, after they had secluded themselves in a carriage for nearly three-quarters of an hour and had only come out once more than one person had pounded upon the carriage door . . . well, society was simply waiting on pins and needles to learn what would come of the two next. Most were shocked Sir Mulgrave hadn't demanded they be taken to Gretna Green immediately. That they exited the carriage and immediately declared their engagement had, at least, quelled most of the meanest gossipmongers.

She smiled as Eliza and Lord Lambert moved from one acquaintance to another. Miss Kitty remained by their side, usually holding Eliza's hand and periodically hugging her for no apparent reason. The little girl was clearly as overjoyed as the rest of them regarding the impending nuptials.

Charlotte caught sight of Sir Mulgrave coming her way. Instantly, all the flutterings she'd been trying to ignore for weeks came back in force. What was it about that man that forever grated against her?

Sir Mulgrave walked up toward her, even stood shoulder to shoulder with her, but didn't speak.

She waited, wishing she could win their silent battle by holding out longer until she could bear it no longer.

"Eliza looks radiant tonight," she said.

"That she does." That the man cherished his daughter was evident in his voice.

They stood silent for several more minutes, he, slowly sipping at the drink in his hand, she, watching the people passing by them but not truly seeing a single one.

"Listen," Sir Mulgrave said at length. "It's been made perfectly clear that we're both a bit stubborn."

"Stubborn?" He had the gall to call her such?

He lifted a hand. "We *both* are."

She let out a small huff but didn't disagree.

"So," his voice grew softer as he continued, "I say we reconcile." With a brief cough, his tone turned back to full volume. "Just for the benefit of the girls."

"*Just* for the girls?"

"Of course."

Well, she would be lying if she didn't admit she was tired of their stand-off. "All right. Let us put what has been said in the past and move on."

"Good."

Charlotte eyed Sir Mulgrave. If she wasn't mistaken, that was no small amount of relief she'd heard in his tone.

"Furthermore," he said, "I want to thank you. If not for you, Eliza would not be so happily situated."

"He'll be good to her," Charlotte said, her gaze moving toward the happy couple, even as a smile grew on her face. "And she'll be a lovely wife."

"That she will," Sir Mulgrave said, emotion once more slipping into his tone.

"Lady Augusta has been quite gracious, all things considered." It was perhaps a bit of an unimportant on-dit, but Charlotte found herself wanting to continue the conversation with Sir Mulgrave, no matter the topic. "Her parents, too. They told me quite plainly they fault neither Eliza nor the family in any way."

"Have they left Town, then?"

"Yes, and just in time. News of their eldest daughter's choice reached London not twelve hours after they departed. Though I know Eliza is sad her friend is not with her tonight, I agree with Lord and Lady Honeyfield that taking Augusta away was best for her."

"Do you suppose all will be well for her next Season?"

Charlotte smiled a bit—Sir Mulgrave had never been one to care about gossip. Was it wrong for her to hope he was simply wanting to speak with her as much as she was wanting to speak with him?

"I believe so," Charlotte said. "Her father enjoys many connections in Town, and I am determined to do all I can for her next year. I am fully confident Lady Augusta will be nothing less than the diamond of the Season."

Sir Mulgrave only nodded, but she caught sight of his approval in the way the corner of his mouth ticked upward.

"Speaking of next year," Charlotte said slowly, turning her gaze back toward Lord Lambert and Eliza, "now that you are assured one son-in-law, you could return home." Even as she said it, however, the words brought a small pang to her chest. One she quickly ignored and shoved away.

"But what of Rachel and Dinah?"

"Lord Lambert would be more than willing to host them next year for another Season, I'm sure." Though she knew better than to bring it up, she was not blind to the fact that this trip was costing all the resources that should have been diverted toward seeing Sir Mulgrave situated for life. If he left now, it would be far easier for him to secure a parcel of land big enough for him to live comfortably off of.

"Nonsense," he muttered under his breath. "A true father does not leave his own daughters' welfare in the hands of another man—not even their own brother-in-law."

Despite the use of the dreaded 'nonsense,' Charlotte still

warmed at his words. "You're a good man, Sir Mulgrave."

"Don't get me wrong. I sincerely wish I *could* return to the country."

The pang returned. But so did Charlotte's determination to ignore it.

"I'm worried for Rachel," Sir Mulgrave continued. "Eliza at least made a few friends when first we arrived. But Rachel hasn't made any. And Dinah"—he let out a grunt—"she's made far too many of the wrong types of friends."

Yes, Charlotte had begun to worry for both girls. Even now, Rachel stood near the back of the room alone, while Dinah fluttered her lashes at Lord Down.

"I keep telling her to stay away from that man," Sir Mulgrave said, his tone tense. "The more I push, the angrier she gets." He shook his head. "I've never had this problem with any of my girls before."

"Well, then," Charlotte spoke, even as the idea came to her, "what if I proposed a change of scenery?"

"Aren't we in Town for the *whole* Season?"

"There are still many, many months to go. It would not be strange or thought ill of if we took a trip out to the country for a month or two."

Sir Mulgrave's lips pulled to one side, even as he muttered, "Nonsensical rich people."

She swatted him on the shoulder—hard. "If you're going to take that attitude, I will leave you all to your fate. Here in London. With *him*." She pointed at Lord Down.

"Country air, you say?" Sir Mulgrave turned toward her, smiling. "A change of society?"

Charlotte took her win but didn't crow over him for it. They still were not on the best footing with one another. "My dear friend lives not half a day's journey from here. She has a lovely country home and is always eager for visitors. More still, she has a grandson who's recently returned from his Grand Tour, and I think his temperament might be just what Rachel needs to break her out of her quiet shell."

"Rachel has always preferred a smaller gathering, just as Eliza has."

Just as you have, but Charlotte kept that to herself. "Yes, I quite think your girls will find it delightful."

"And," he said leaning in closer, "*certain* men won't be there?"

"I can guarantee it. Lord Down is not the least bit acquainted with the Dowager Fitzwilliam."

"Done." Sir Mulgrave emptied the contents of his glass. "Shall we leave tomorrow?"

Charlotte laughed. "Let me at least write the dear woman first and let her know we are on our way."

He let out a sigh in mock frustration. "Very well."

He came across all prickles and thorns, and yet underneath was a man who was willing to risk his own future to safeguard his daughters'. A man who did occasionally joke. She was glad she would be able to spend more time with Sir Mulgrave—it had been a very long time since she'd met a man as puzzling as him.

"I'll go tell the girls now," she said. He bowed and she curtsied, and they moved separate directions.

Of a truth, Charlotte's life had been ever so much better since that day Sir Mulgrave had stopped the highwaymen. Not only had his courage saved her, but being a benefactress to his daughters had filled her life in a way she hadn't known she needed. She loved her son dearly, but she'd always wanted a daughter. Now, in a way, she had three. It was selfish, but she was very happy Sir Mulgrave wasn't packing up and calling it quits just yet. She wasn't ready to give up her new family.

Charlotte reached Rachel and draped an arm over her shoulders. "My dear, your father and I were just speaking, and guess what we have decided to do?"

The End
The romance continues in
The Determined Miss Rachel

He's been waiting months for her to finally notice him.
Except suddenly, he's not the only one vying for her hand.

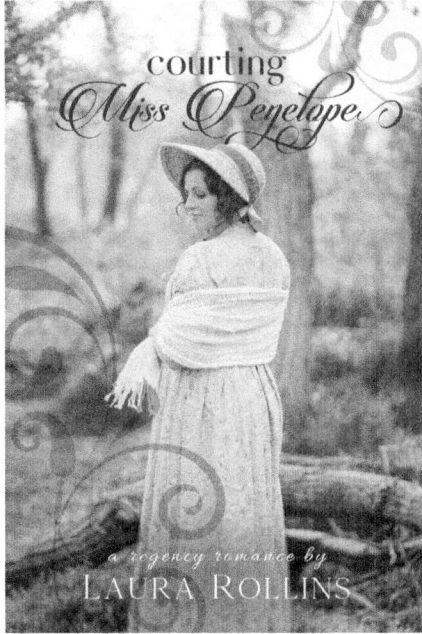

Download the short story for free at:
www.LauraRollins.com

DISCUSSION QUESTIONS

- When Seth Mulgrave saved Lady Blackmore from the highwaymen, it was an act of physical bravery. Eliza, on the other hand, demonstrated what could be called emotional or social bravery. Do you feel that kind of bravery also takes courage? Or would you not label it as "courage", but as something else?
- Compare standing up when the consequence might be physical pain and standing up when the consequences might be social ridicule. Is one easier or harder for you? Do you feel you would be more likely to do one over the other?
- Audacious is considered a synonym for Courageous. However, like all synonyms, there are subtle differences between these two words. What do you think of when you hear the word Courage? Now, what do you think of when you hear the word Audacious? In what ways do you feel these words are synonyms and in what ways are they different?
- Eliza struggles to voice her own needs and opinions; she

often worries that she will inadvertently hurt another if she focuses on herself. Have you ever struggled with this? What ways have you found to balance helping others and seeing to your own needs?

ACKNOWLEDGMENTS

No book is ever written without much encouragement and support from any number of people. I am forever thankful to my husband and children, as their patience and love is the reason I get to do this.

Special thanks go to my writing groups, for their advice and help. Also to Jenny Proctor and Emily Poole; without your suggestions and edits this book would not have been half so good.

Lastly, thanks to my Father in Heaven, for giving me a beautiful life and the opportunity to create.

ABOUT THE AUTHOR

Laura Rollins has always loved a heart-melting happily ever after. It didn't matter if the story took place in Regency England, in outer space, beneath the Earth's crust, or in a cobbler's shop, if there was a sweet romance, she would read it.

Life has given her many of her own adventures. Currently she lives in the Rocky Mountains with her best-friend, who is also her husband, and their four beautiful children. She still loves to read books and more books; her favorite types of music are classical, Broadway, and country; she'd rather be hiking the mountains than twiddling her thumbs on the beach; and she's been known to debate with her oldest son over whether Infinity is better categorized as a number or an idea.

For more books, updates,
and a free short story, check out:
www.LauraRollins.com

Printed in Great Britain
by Amazon